Nico stared down at her with dark, smoldering eyes

"Damn, but you're hot."

Lainie reached out for him impatiently. "How would you know when you're not even close enough to touch?"

He fell on her with a speed that would have done his sport proud. God knows it pleased her no end. He stretched out next to her on the lounger, molding his body to hers as they lay on their sides, facing each another. His hand tugged down the zipper on her skirt. "How about this? Is this close enough?"

"Not nearly, and you know it." She wriggled her hips to ease the zipper down all the faster. "Don't start something you can't finish."

Steering the skirt over her hips and down her thighs, he stared into her eyes as if he could see every secret hidden inside her. "Don't worry about me finishing. I'm just going to make sure that it's you who finishes first."

Blaze™

Dear Reader,

When I first conceived the idea for the SINGLE IN SOUTH BEACH series, I paired off Brianne, Summer and Giselle—three of the owners of Club Paradise—pretty quickly. But then I looked at the last co-owner, burned-by-love divorcée Lainie Reynolds, and wondered who I could put in her path that would inspire her to take a second chance. The resort CEO and diva of South Beach would steamroll over the average man in no time.

Luckily, Giselle Cesare had a wealth of arrogant, in-your-face brothers running around Miami, and I chose Nico, the wild hockey player, to turn Lainie's head. I hope you'll agree these two make a fun couple, although get ready for some serious sparks to fly! This is one heroine who isn't wading back into romance easily.

I hope you'll join me for next month's SINGLE IN SOUTH BEACH story. *Her Final Fling* will be a July Harlequin Temptation novel, and we'll see what's in store for Nico's older brother Vito. Visit me at www.JoanneRock.com to learn more about my future releases!

Happy reading,

Joanne Rock

Books by Joanne Rock

HARLEQUIN BLAZE

26—SILK, LACE & VIDEOTAPE
48—IN HOT PURSUIT
54—WILD AND WILLING
87—WILD AND WICKED
104—SEX & THE SINGLE GIRL*
108—GIRL'S GUIDE TO HUNTING
    & KISSING*
135—GIRL GONE WILD*

*Single in South Beach

HARLEQUIN TEMPTATION

863—LEARNING CURVES
897—TALL, DARK AND DARING
919—REVEALED
951—ONE NAUGHTY NIGHT

HARLEQUIN HISTORICALS

694—THE WEDDING KNIGHT

DATE WITH A DIVA

Joanne Rock

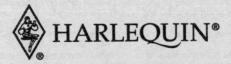

HARLEQUIN®

TORONTO • NEW YORK • LONDON
AMSTERDAM • PARIS • SYDNEY • HAMBURG
STOCKHOLM • ATHENS • TOKYO • MILAN • MADRID
PRAGUE • WARSAW • BUDAPEST • AUCKLAND

For the wonderfully supportive folks at Harlequin who make following my writing dream such a continuous pleasure. In particular, I can't send enough thanks to the art department for the fabulous covers, the marketing and public relations departments for sending my stories across the globe, the production department for refining my word choices on those occasions when my tongue gets tangled and the editorial department for providing such a fantastic venue for series romance.

And for Dean, who is especially helpful when it comes to offering insights on the mind of the male athlete.
Thank you for the ten-year hockey education, and oh yeah—Go Penguins!

ISBN 0-373-79143-7

DATE WITH A DIVA

Copyright © 2004 by Joanne Rock.

Prologue

CREATING TROUBLE in Club Paradise:

1. Initiate personnel problems among the staff.
2. Lay the groundwork for an explosive situation.
3. Publicize the whole mess on network television, or better yet—a full-length feature film.
4. Force The Diva—ice princess Lainie Reynolds—to remember my name.

The disgruntled Club Paradise guest crossed off the first item on the list while listening to the argument brewing in the hallway just outside one of the exotic hotel's kitchens. The lush South Beach singles' resort would rapidly lose credibility without a chef, and from the sounds of things, the new cook wouldn't last the rest of the day.

Pencil hovering above the second task on the list, the intruder peered across the kitchen to the half-prepared food strewn across a counter beside the stainless-steel sink. No sense being premature about scratching the explosion item off the list. With any luck, all hell would break loose soon anyhow.

For now, everything was right on schedule.

Just the way uptight perfectionist Lainie Reynolds liked it.

1

ALONE AT LAST.

When she'd finally put a good thirty blocks between her and Club Paradise, CEO Lainie Reynolds found a bench near the ocean and let out the breath she'd been holding ever since she stormed out of the hotel. Always conscious of her image, she hadn't wanted to be near anyone she worked with when she allowed the stress from her hellacious day to flood through her.

Setting down the flask of Kentucky bourbon on the wooden bench beside her, she let her frustrations hiss between her teeth in the form of an extended sigh.

Damn Robert Flynn.

She'd been divorced from him for almost a year now, so she hadn't expected her ex-husband's preliminary hearing to prey so heavily on her heart. Hell, she'd helped put the bastard behind bars after he'd cheated on her with a gorgeous younger woman, then proceeded to cheat their friends and business associates out of millions of dollars. He'd embezzled money from the resort she'd held a small share in and later reorganized, so essentially he'd stolen from her, too. He'd also cleaned out their checking account and used some of her personal money to buy up local real estate and sell it for his own profit before he skipped town.

Her divorce had been bitter to say the least.

Indulging in another nip from the elegant flask she'd

never had cause to use until now, Lainie breathed in the moist, salty air and willed herself to relax. She needed the soothing peace of a quiet stretch of ocean to process everything that had happened today.

The news of Robert's hearing had hit her hard, but she hadn't been able to think through it with a film crew arriving at the resort to start production of a new movie this week. Having Club Paradise featured in the sexiest new action-adventure drama to be released next year could really put them on the international map.

But her life was such a screwed-up mess she wouldn't be able to make the most of the opportunity unless she pulled herself together. On top of that, it would be torturous to be around all those steamy scenes in progress while her own love life sucked.

Only when her heart rate slowed did she allow herself to drag today's paper out of her purse.

Fallen Flynn Held Without Bail.

There was a mug shot of Robert Flynn, her cheating ex, beside the headline. Underneath that picture there was a photo of her and Robert at a charity gala last spring, a huge Miami society event that had been sponsored by her law firm. It had been the beginning of the end for them since she'd caught him canoodling with some paralegal from her company during the silent auction portion of the evening. One of many in a long line of women, she discovered later.

Her eyes had been irrevocably opened that night after years of denial. But when the newspaper photo had been taken, that awful moment of realization hadn't happened yet. Lainie was clutching Robert's hand with the mindless conviction of someone who needed to be right about her choices no matter what the cost. She'd never been a clingy woman, but she'd always been certain that whatever she chose must be right by sheer virtue of the fact that she'd made the decision.

So damn full of herself.

Lainie picked up the flask again, promising herself this would be her last sip. She was a one-or-two glass kind of woman, refusing to ever succumb to a state of being where she would be out of control. Sloppy. Or worst of all, stupid.

Savoring the burn in her throat from that last swig even as she crammed the flask back in her purse, she was surprised to see tears fall on the newspaper she held in her lap.

He deserved to be in jail. She *wanted* him in jail, damn it. She just hadn't counted on how much the confirmation of his criminal activity in black and white would make her feel like a first-class failure.

Grateful she'd escaped Club Paradise before she lost it, Lainie let the tears dot the newsprint. Sure she'd recovered financially from the whole disaster—she'd left her law practice and ended up taking over Club Paradise with the help of three partners. They'd shifted the focus of the resort from a schmaltzy couples' love nest to a sleek, sensuous playground for singles, and met with phenomenal success.

But in all the months she'd struggled to put the business in the black, Lainie had never once stopped to put her heart back in order. Damn. Damn. Damn.

Folding and unfolding the newspaper in her lap, Lainie allowed the hurt of Robert's betrayal to wash over her. She'd always hated being the butt of a joke, and now she seemed to be a full-blown source of public ridicule. Even now during her anonymous minibinge on the beach she felt people's eyes on her, as if they were pointing and staring behind her back. Ridiculous.

She would indulge the pity party for ten more minutes and then she'd get back to business. Back to her one-track life.

But as she stared down at the front page of the *Miami Herald*, Lainie spied a pair of men's worn leather loafers out of the corner of her eye. Great. Just what she didn't need. Witnesses to the damn pity party.

Apparently there were eyes on her after all. With any luck, those eyes belonged to someone who didn't have a damn clue about her hideous mistake.

Thankfully, the shoes stepped back again, away from her and her personal dark cloud. But just as she breathed a sigh of relief, the shoes came back. Closer. Paused.

Irritated, Lainie arranged her features in a death stare guaranteed to set any man on his ass. As she lifted her chin and spied the rest of the loafer owner, however, it occurred to her there might be better uses for this particular man's ass.

A marathon sack session immediately sprang to mind.

He had the body of an athlete, which couldn't be disguised by his khaki shorts and black polo shirt with some kind of panther logo on the pocket. From the mouthwatering definition of his pecs against the cotton fabric, she just knew he'd have amazing abs under that shirt. At a few inches over six foot, he had long arms and legs, bronzed and sprinkled with dark hair, thanks to some sort of Mediterranean heritage.

And, yes, after she noticed the body that looked as if it could go all night long, she did also take a glance at his face. With his thick dark hair and long eyelashes framing gorgeous brown eyes, he would have been way too pretty if not for a nose that had seen the wrong end of too many fistfights. Two distinct crooks could have been borderline disfiguring on anyone else, but they gave this guy a certain all-male, don't-mess-with-me appeal.

"Lainie?"

So much for anonymous.

She shook off her frank observation of the interloper, wondering where all that female interest had come from. She hadn't noticed any man that way since…before she got married.

Welcome back, hormones.

Still, as nice as it might be to know she could experience the itch, she wasn't in any mood for scratching today. "I'm sorry. Do I know you?"

Scavenging for some semblance of the death stare, she settled for a mild glare. No matter how enticing this newcomer might be, she really needed to be alone today until she could rein in her messy emotions.

"I'm Nico." He said it with the certainty of a man who knew his identity would explain everything.

"I'm usually good with names, but—"

"Nico Cesare. Giselle's brother?" He sounded vaguely put out. That was the problem with good-looking men. They thought they were too memorable to forget.

Giselle Cesare was one of four partners that owned controlling shares of Club Paradise. She and Lainie had their differences since Giselle had slept with Lainie's ex-husband—*before* they'd divorced. Very messy situation all around. Their partnership had been hideously tense until they'd joined forces in a mini-sting operation to bring Robert Flynn to justice.

And come to think of it, there had been another guy

who'd waltzed onto the scene the day they'd brought down Robert.

She snapped her fingers as she recalled the man's face.

"You were there the day they arrested my ex." The memory blindsided her with sudden clarity. She'd put the event out of her mind until today's newspaper had hit her desk.

His expression softened. "When Giselle's boyfriend asked me for backup, how could I refuse a chance to bring down the pissant crook who screwed over my sister?" As he shrugged, his square shoulders drew her eye. "No offense."

Lainie let the old anger roll over her. Off her. "Robert Flynn has already offended me more than any one woman deserves. I think I'm impervious to your run-of-the mill slights and slurs."

"But I didn't mean—"

"You didn't mean to imply I married a blight on humanity? Of course you did. And how can I penalize you for an honest observation?"

"Touchy subject?" He reached in his pocket and withdrew some sort of orange-and-purple beanbag. Whatever it was, he squeezed the fabric back and forth between his fingers in an almost unconscious gesture.

"Not at all." She folded the newspaper article in half, unwilling to let him see she'd been wasting even ten minutes mourning her failed marriage to a criminal. She peered around the beach in an effort to change the subject. "You live around here?"

"No. I just happened to be in the neighborhood. I thought I recognized you from Club Paradise and I—" he worked the little orange-and-purple sack in his hand faster "—thought I shouldn't let you drink alone."

Crap.

"You saw me hitting the bottle?" Now the only man who'd awakened her hibernating hormones in years thought she was a closet drunk. Probably just as well since she had no business drooling over Giselle's too handsome brother anyhow. And hadn't her friend said all her brothers were overprotective and chauvinistic? Thanks, but no thanks.

"It seemed a little incongruous for a businesswoman wearing white linen to go for the flask in the middle of a public beach." He jerked his thumb in the direction of her bench. "Mind if I join you?"

"Why? So you can make sure your sister's business partner doesn't go on a bender in full view of the all-important Miami tourist crowd?"

"Um. No." Nico swiveled his head around to glance up and down the beach. "I read the paper today, too. And in my family, we don't let each other drink alone."

A pause stretched between them. His words flustered her more than she would let on, but maybe that was just because she felt like an emotional basket case today. And, damn it, since when were good-looking guys also thoughtful? Maybe she was just disconcerted because he insisted on playing against type.

"You're welcome to have a seat." She scooted over a few inches to make sure they wouldn't be too close. "But since we're not family, you don't need to risk your liver for me."

"Trust me, I've taxed my liver for far less worthy causes." He lowered himself to the bench, which was a long way down for a man so damn tall. "I got blitzed once so our star forward could tell his wife it had been me who trashed their house at a team party. We thought a vodka-induced stupor might make the story more believable and, sure enough, she bought it.''

"Another woman deceived. How noble." Any warmth Lainie might have felt at his mission not to let her drink alone vanished.

"Stupid, wasn't it? She was eight months pregnant at the time and I thought I'd be the good guy by smoothing over another player's mistake." He shook his head as he tossed the orange-and-purple object he'd been holding into the air. A Hacky Sack. She remembered seeing kids kick a beanbag like that from foot to foot on playgrounds.

"But I only staved off the inevitable," Nico continued, tossing and catching the sack while hardly sparing a glance for the action. "The guy couldn't handle fame and fortune, let alone a wife and kid. Yvonne would have been better off knowing what a shit she'd married straight out of the gate."

"Amen." Lainie didn't bother informing him that sometimes women were well aware of their spouses' shortcomings—they were simply too proud to admit them. Or did that particular stubborn streak only apply to her? "So what is all this talk of a team and star forwards? You play basketball?"

Her sports knowledge was nonexistent, but she'd dated a Michael Jordan fan in her pre-Robert Flynn era, and she was pretty sure forwards went with hoops. Maybe.

He snagged his Hacky Sack out of the air and clutched his chest as if she'd dealt him a blow. "Damn that hurts. Giselle doesn't ever talk about her brothers? Hell, I brag to everyone I meet what a great chef she is and how she owns a piece of Club Paradise. She never so much as breathed a word to her partners about her brother playing hockey?''

"Given the rocky start to our partnership, Giselle and I pretty much stuck to business whenever we were forced to speak to one another until recently.'' They'd launched a kick-ass singles' resort with the help of their partners Brianne Wolcott and Summer Farnsworth. "Where do you play hockey?''

"Played. Past tense.'' Nico stared out at the ocean and she recognized the tension humming through his body. The leashed desire to rage at the world. "I used to play with the Florida Panthers before I pulled my hamstring and became washed up at thirty-two. Now I'm a second-rate coach on the team I took to the Stanley Cup finals.''

"I won't pretend to know anything about sports, but I'm sure that sucks.'' Lainie wondered if he realized he had the Hacky Sack strangled in a death grip.

"And that was just the start of my year. Speaking of which, where did you hide that flask?''

Lainie debated the wisdom of spending any more time in his company. She felt more than a little vulnerable out here with all her usual boundaries thrown aside. The bourbon singing in her veins kept telling her she deserved some company, but her better judgment knew she couldn't afford any hot and heavy interlude when she was still on the rebound.

Maybe as long as she didn't allow herself to get sucked in by those dark, brooding eyes, she'd be okay.

"I don't mind sharing my stash, Cesare.'' She reached for the flask and handed it over with a flourish. Bourbon loosening her tongue, she couldn't help drawing boundaries early on. "But consider yourself forewarned—just because we share a drink doesn't mean I'm going home with you.''

NOTHING LIKE COMING STRAIGHT to the point.

But then, in the weeks that he'd been watching Lainie Reynolds, Nico had learned a man needed an iron-fortified ego to withstand the likes of the Club Paradise CEO.

The shrewd Miami attorney-turned-businesswoman had a reputation for plowing through obstacles, focusing on her goals with single-minded determination. They called her the "Diva" behind her back, but anyone who wanted to do business with her tended to call her ma'am.

Luckily for Nico, the required hearty ego didn't present a problem. A damn good thing since he wanted Lainie. Badly.

"I appreciate the heads up on the sleeping arrangements. Or lack thereof." He took the proffered container, holding her gaze as his fingers grazed hers. She had damn warm fingers for a cool, remote diva. "I trust you'll let me know if you change your mind on that?"

As someone who held the record for most shutouts in a hockey season in the NHL, he wasn't used to being refused. Not that he'd ever been the kind of guy to pursue women for sport, but normally if he was interested, so was the female in question. Even now that his career as a star goalie was in the toilet, he still attracted plenty of recognition. Attention. Women.

Except for this one.

"You'll definitely be the first to know." She retracted her fingers, seeming to retreat from him mentally, too. But then, he'd known from the start she was having a bad day since he'd followed her all the way from the resort late this afternoon.

He'd been on the property to oversee a few things for his sister since she'd taken off to Europe with her new boyfriend. Giselle had left her position as executive chef, carefully hiring her replacement before she went overseas, but she'd wanted to be sure the woman's adjustment went smoothly, given that Lainie Reynolds was a notoriously tough boss.

Nico had meant to get around to checking on the club, but he'd had five other things to do at the club and he'd gotten distracted when he'd spotted Lainie storming out of the hotel shortly after six o'clock— early in the day for a big-time workaholic. He'd followed her on instinct.

With medium height and a fairly average female build, there was nothing physically tangible he could point to about Lainie Reynolds that had captured his attention. But there was something about the force of her personality that came through in her ramrod-straight posture and her smooth, efficient way of moving. Shoulder-length blond hair grazed a white linen jacket that looked as if it wouldn't dare wrinkle while she wore it. Her short white skirt was pencil slim and showed off legs that hadn't seen much sun despite the relentless Florida weather.

He didn't know her well, but she'd snagged his eye last month when she'd joined forces with his sister to put Lainie's embezzling ex-husband behind bars. Nico had arrived on the scene to find Ms. Corporate Lainie decked out in full ass-kicking regalia, from steel-toed boots to eye-popping leather pants that had invaded his dreams ever since. He'd be hard-pressed ever to look at Ms. Corporate in the same way again.

Too bad she'd barely taken note of him. Then or now.

But if Nico had anything to say about it, that was all about to change.

2

"GO ON, SLICK. Do your worst." She gestured to the flask he still held in his hand. "I've already had my share for today."

Nico took a deep breath and called himself back from fantasies about this woman. If he wanted a shot with her, he needed to be on his toes. As he'd followed her up Ocean Drive today, walking a half block behind her, he'd slowly formulated a plan. He had two more months in the off-season to get his life in order and figure out if he wanted to keep the coaching gig he hated. Until then, he'd further his sister's interests at Club Paradise while furthering his own very personal interest in Ms. Lainie Reynolds.

"You can't be done. You took what—two sips? What kind of enabler would I be if I let you off the hook with that?" He took a swig and nearly fried his throat. "Jesus, woman, what have you got in here?" His words croaked with the firepower of her beverage of choice.

She didn't smile, but he could see the hint of humor in her eyes. He'd been watching her on and off at Club Paradise over the last few weeks. In that time, Nico had never caught Lainie in a full-out grin.

"It's homemade Kentucky bourbon." She came damn close to smiling when he coughed. "I know it's not exactly smooth, but it's—sentimental."

"No way in hell you're a Kentucky girl." His re-action leaped out of his mouth before he had a chance to weigh the pros and cons. A frequent, unhappy affliction of his since childhood.

"I may be a big-shot Miami businesswoman, but everyone has a past." All traces of smiles and shared humor disappeared as she looked out to sea. The sunset painted the water warm pinks and oranges, giving the whole beach a surreal glow. Even Lainie's shoulder-length blond hair was tinged strawberry.

"What were you saying about yours, Cesare?" she prodded. "You lost your spot on the hockey team and then what?"

He'd been hoping for commiseration, not interrogation. But he had the feeling that if he wanted to keep his place next to her, he needed to put himself out there.

"I'll spill the whole sordid story if you share the bourbon and whatever's got you down today."

"You go crazy with the bourbon." She waved him on with a hurry-up gesture. "I know it well enough to respect it."

"Hey, I've had a shit year, too." He took another, more careful sip of the bourbon. This time he could better taste the appeal. It wasn't smooth, but there was a hell of a kick. "I'm not above a little comfort where I can find it." He peered across the bench at her again. "And you did make it clear I wouldn't be finding it with you tonight, correct?"

One side of her mouth hitched up. Not a smile. More like a wry smirk. Still, he counted it as progress.

"Correct." She eyed him as he leaned his head back against the bench. "But if we were to debate who deserves comfort of any kind here, I think I've still got you beat.''

''Ah, but you haven't heard my story yet. The gut-wrenching drama of professional sports, complete with passion, fame, heartbreak… It's practically a prime-time special in the making.'' He didn't want to push too hard, but he didn't want her to leave now that they were finally talking. He'd been waiting for weeks to get this close to her. Failure was not an option. He hadn't been interested in the chase since Ashley booted him out after his career ended. For the first time since then his hormones were on full alert.

And yeah, maybe after watching his career go up in smoke and his love life land in the crapper, he liked the idea of slaying some dragons for a lady. In spite of her tough exterior, he could see Lainie had more than a few shadowy demons lurking in her eyes right now.

''Then bring it on, superstar. Your story and the bourbon.'' She gestured for her flask with an impatient waggle of her fingers. Her nails gleamed with dark copper polish, each one as long and perfectly shaped as the next. ''If we're serious about drowning our sorrows, I'd better have a few more sips. I've never been the sort of woman to do anything by half measures.''

He handed over the flask. ''Damn but you're scary. No wonder Giselle spent all year hiding from you.''

''Is that right?'' Her eyebrows rose as if she was enjoying a compliment. She stole a sip of her backwoods brew without a wince. ''It's a skill carefully cultivated by ambulance chasers. I'm not in that business any longer, but you know what they say about old habits. However, we are *not* talking about me tonight.''

Yet.

Nico wasn't about to let her off the hook without

finding out more about her, but he'd honor the deal they'd made.

"Okay, chapter one—my hamstring shreds in a combination of old muscle problems and a skate blade to the back of my thigh. I'm out of the game for good."

"Just like that?" She crossed her legs, distracting him with the shifting of slim thighs against her short white skirt. "No second opinions from other doctors?"

"Actually, this is after ten different opinions from hapless doctors who are thanked by me raging and shaking my fist. I guess I omitted the part where I act like a two-year-old and endear myself to no one." Nico watched as she smoothed the hemline of her already straight skirt. Memories of her in tight black leather blared into his brain, the same mental pictures that had haunted him ever since the night she and Giselle told Robert Flynn where to get off.

Nico had been getting off on the memory for weeks.

"Didn't you have a contract?" Her question forced him to blink away the black leather.

"Absolutely. But in my egomania at the time, I signed a one-year deal knowing I'd have a monster season of career highs and then I'd be in a position to sign a longer deal for more money." Stupid, selfish move, but then he'd always been the kind of guy to go for it all and put himself on the line. If he hadn't been thinking about having a record-breaking deal quoted on ESPN, he would have just gone for the very reasonable long-term option the Panthers had offered him. He'd chosen to gamble.

"So you're bummed because after years of living on the big-league paycheck, you're back to nothing once your contract year is up." She took another sip and passed the bottle back. When he set his Hacky Sack down to take the flask, she nodded at his new toy. "May I?"

"Sure." He couldn't picture her playing Hacky Sack but he handed it over. "Only I wasn't upset about the money so much as the lost glory. Hockey is—was— my whole life. You remember *Field of Dreams* and how the people in the movie were so nuts for baseball?" He waited for her nod. "That's how I am about hockey. It's—it *was*—a way of life."

Pointing one of her perfectly painted fingernails at him, she stared him down. "I hope you've already talked to a financial planner."

Bad enough he was spilling his guts, he'd be damned if he would take financial advice, too. He made a noncommittal shrug.

"Okay. After six years in corporate law, I had to at least warn you. Chapter two?" She squeezed the Hacky Sack between her fingers the same way that he liked to when he wasn't kicking the hell out of the thing.

Distracted by her hands, he was surprised when she handed the beanbag back to him.

"Chapter two?" She prodded like an impatient trial lawyer nudging the witness.

Nico wondered if she would be that aggressive in bed. And if he'd ever have a chance to find out for himself.

"Chapter two finds me without a job, which quickly leads to my girlfriend walking out."

"She sure wasn't much of a girlfriend."

"I didn't discover until too late that groupies are only interested in the fame and the paycheck." Although Ashley had done a hell of a job convincing him they wanted the same things in life—kids, family, roots. He'd laid his heart on the line for her, too, only to have it booted back to him. "To be fair, though, I guess I'd always been pretty interested in the fame and the paycheck, too."

"And not to stick up for this piranha of a girlfriend, but is there any chance you were just flat out bad company once your luck changed?" She recrossed her legs in the other direction, calling his attention to the lean thighs that he'd been dreaming about for weeks. "Sometimes people can turn superornery when the rug has been pulled out from under them."

"I'm positive I acted like a complete bastard at times, but I thought our relationship was more grounded than that." Ashley leaving him had been a second slap in the face—no, make that a third—after his injury and his career ending.

"You think maybe you could work things out now that you've leveled out? Assuming you have?"

Yeah, sure he was level. Most of the time. "Nope. She's dating my replacement on the team."

"Ouch."

"Apparently my judgment sucks."

"So does mine." She lifted the flask to toast him. "Looks like we have something in common."

If he'd had a drink of his own, Nico would have chugged long and thoroughly to that notion. He promised himself it would be the first of many things they had in common.

As it stood, he settled for watching Lainie's lips mold around the top of the bourbon bottle and imagining what they'd feel like wrapped around him. Soon.

"Cheers to common ground. Now it's your turn for some storytelling."

LAINIE BLINKED and the movement seemed to take forever.

She struggled to haul her eyelids back up, eager to feast her gaze on the tall, dark and delectable Nico Cesare again.

"Lainie?" He even *sounded* gorgeous.

"Hmm?" As she licked her lips and tasted the bourbon her grandfather had given her as a going-away present when she left Kentucky, Lainie remembered she was already getting drunk tonight. Bad enough she'd let naughty Nico talk her into wallowing in her sorrows, leading to the pleasant numbing effects of alcohol. She definitely couldn't indulge in sex with a stranger.

"Are you okay?" His voice was all concern and deep male bass.

She could eat him up with a spoon if the timing had been different. If she hadn't been confronted with her own failure on page one of the *Herald* today.

"I'm fine." She passed him the bottle back and let her eyes linger on those well-muscled arms of his. Without her permission her gaze fell to his chest. His muscular thighs. "Too fine, in fact. I don't think I'd better have any more."

"You want to start walking back toward the hotel while I coerce your story out of you?" He looked around the beach. "We're a long way from Club Paradise up here."

Lainie bit back the first thought in her head—that they should get a room at the nearest hotel instead. She never knew bourbon was an aphrodisiac.

"Good idea." Rising carefully to make sure she didn't fall over when she stood, Lainie handed him the newspaper she'd been holding. "And if you want my story, all you need to do is read today's paper."

Without sparing it a glance, he shot the newspaper into a waste can at the end of the bench. "That's your ex-husband's story—a guy who didn't know how to hold on to a good thing." His dark eyes latched onto hers in the twilight. "I want to know what's bothering you enough to make you come out here all by yourself and drink some sentimental concoction that could peel the paint off your nails. You don't really miss that guy, do you?"

Somehow seeing the paper in the trash made her feel marginally better.

"Of course I don't miss him." She did miss the idea of being married even though she'd never admit it. There was a certain respectability that came with marriage. And comfort.

"I just hate that I'm going to cringe for the rest of my life whenever I have to talk about my ex-husband, the convicted criminal." She tried to shrug it off as if it was no big deal. Obviously she didn't want to get into the whys and wherefores of how her marriage weighed on her like a giant red F—a grade she'd always feared but never actually received in school. She'd never fully shaken her backwoods roots. The sense of being watched and judged followed her around even now.

She swayed on her feet a little as she put her leather sandals back on. Nico's arm snaked around her waist to steady her. Of course, having him stand that close to her did little to stabilize her. If anything, she only felt more light-headed.

"The guy's a professional scammer who sucked in thousands of investors all over the state. It only makes sense he'd be damn good at putting on a front and making you believe whatever he wanted you to believe.''

"So all that stuff Robert spouted about love and happily ever after was just for show? Gee, Nico, you're really cheering me up." She finally managed to jam both of her feet into her sandals, then she edged out of his grip to test her balance.

Still standing.

Still standing.

Falling!

Strong arms gripped her waist and steadied her spine. She found herself plastered against the wall of muscle that served as Nico's chest and, oh my, wasn't that nice.

Her linen suit jacket had edged open just enough to stay out of the way. Only his cotton T-shirt and her silk tank top separated them. Okay, technically she had a bra on under there, too, but she'd been wearing skimpy French lingerie all year in an effort to reawaken her hormones and affirm her sense that, damn it, yes, she was still an attractive woman even if her idiot ex-husband ran around with perky-breasted bimbos. Well, except for Giselle, who was definitely perky but not a bimbo.

But the gossamer-thin silk of her bra wasn't exactly a barrier between her and Nico's hot bod. If anything, the made-for-pleasure garment only inspired sexy fantasies about her clothes melting away so this god of a man could see how good she looked in imported undies.

"Sorry about that." Her voice caught in her throat, a rather foreign sensation for a woman who'd built a career around being outspoken.

"I'm not." Nico's fingers fanned out against her back, the broad palms already covering plenty of terrain. "In fact, I can't remember the last time I felt this good."

Me neither. Lainie knew she couldn't fall into his arms. She had zero capacity to think rationally because she was under the influence. Therefore, she couldn't make such a big decision.

But if she could have based the decision on the lust pumping through her right now, she would be wrestling this man's clothes off already.

Her breasts ached against him while her thighs tingled with pleasure to be tangled with his. Heat shot through her to bombard the juncture of her legs...

And damned if she wasn't twitching and wriggling like a cat in heat.

Regret burning her throat, she eased away. "You can't remember the last time?" She tossed his words back at him, taking comfort in confrontation. "Come on, Cesare. You're a hockey star. Women must throw themselves at your feet all the time."

He steadied her shoulders as she wove her way up the beach toward the street. The sooner she got back to the safety—the solitude—of Club Paradise the better.

"Actually, you're the first woman to nearly fall at my feet, but I thought I did a damn good job keeping you upright." His arm remained anchored around her waist as they walked, even though she'd tried to slide away.

Probably just as well. It would be the crowning cap to a hideous day if she fell down on the street because she'd imbibed too much tonight.

Although if she planned her landing just right,

maybe she could find a way to show off that French lingerie when she fell.

"Thank you. I appreciate the hand since it was your dubious advice that inspired me to be such a bad girl tonight." She hadn't meant it to sound like a come-on, but her tone practically dripped a do-me vibe.

He slid a sideways glance at her. "I'm not touching that one."

"Thank you." She gulped and hoped she'd swallowed back whatever wanton demon lurked within her. Although, she had to admit, being bad had never sounded quite so good. "I don't know how it jumped out of my mouth anyway."

"I do. Kentucky bourbon. I'm nominating it as an alternate form of truth serum." His long legs took slow, easy strides that translated into hyperspeed for Lainie. She wasn't a short woman by any stretch of the imagination, but this guy was *tall*. Of course, her stride was inhibited by a slim miniskirt.

They headed left toward Ocean Drive once they neared South Beach. On the north end of Miami Beach, Collins Avenue ran along the water, but as the streets descended, Ocean Drive routed drivers even closer to the shoreline.

"Truth serum?" Lainie chose to focus on her repartee with the arm candy beside her instead of how many more blocks they needed to walk before she could sit down again. Her head was spinning, screwing with her balance, her pulse rate…and her damn overactive hormones. "Maybe we ought to dump a little more of it down your throat then. I think I got robbed on your half of the story. How did you meet the wench who dropped you as soon as you were down on your luck?"

Nico turned his head to the side—sort of down and away from her so she couldn't see his expression. Had she been too insulting? She craned her head across his body to see his face and swayed on her sandals.

His grip tightened around her waist as his chin swiveled toward her again. He smothered a smile. "She's not a wench."

"Whatever. I'm sorry I'm too inebriated to think of more diplomatic names for users." Admiring the way he hadn't sold out his girlfriend, she glanced around the street to get her bearings, fighting a dizzy spell. The heat was killing her and Club Paradise seemed miles away. "Will you stop a minute while I take off my jacket?"

Her escort halted immediately. "You want me to call a cab?" He reached in his shorts pocket and withdrew a phone.

"That's okay." Wriggling her way out of the linen sleeves, she faced the sultry Miami heat in the silk shell she'd worn under her suit. Even now that the sun had set, the pavement still radiated the absorbed warmth of the day. "If I can't make it back, we can just find a bar and get a nightcap to refresh me."

Nico blinked. "I know I must have had too much of that damn brew of yours when an idea like that actually makes sense."

"Do you mean to say you're as pickled as me?"

He eyed her critically. "Probably not."

"I thought big guys had tons of tolerance when it came to alcohol." She continued down the street, knowing she needed to make some serious headway in their trek back to Club Paradise before her liquid knees gave out.

"I always preferred the high of fierce competition."

His arm tightened around her as she walked. "And don't underestimate the alcohol content of that insane backwoods potion you're packing."

She gasped as he tugged her closer, the side of her breast brushing up against his chest somehow. Probably because her arm had found its way around his waist, too. Now when had that happened?

Dizziness assailed her again, and this time she wasn't so sure the bourbon had been at fault. She stopped short, suddenly realizing she couldn't go any farther without addressing the heat wave between them.

"Maybe we'd better get that nightcap I mentioned." Pushing her damp hair from her forehead, she hoped she didn't look like a drunken, sweaty train wreck. She glanced around the street as the dinner crowd began to emerge from local restaurants, ready for more hardcore entertainment. Nightlife sizzled on the strip. "There's a hotel with a bar two doors down."

Nico's eyes widened for a split second before they narrowed to cunning slits. Heat seemed to steam from that dark gaze of his.

"And which exactly are we interested in?" Nico walked her backward toward a telephone booth until they were out of the way of people walking on the street. His hands curved around her waist, his fingers burning right through the sheer fabric of her blouse. The look in his dark eyes was hot enough to make her lick her lips.

"What do you mean?" She barely recognized her breathless voice, and she hoped he wasn't asking what she thought he might be asking because she was in no condition to make an intelligent choice.

His lips loomed above hers, close enough to brush against her own if she arched up just a little bit. Awareness danced over her skin, tingling most in the places her decadent lingerie covered.

"Which are we really looking for right now, Lainie—the hotel or the bar?"

3

A SMARTER MAN wouldn't have pushed the issue. Nico realized that as soon as Lainie and all her sweet curves pulled away from him. A wiser man would have gone with the flow until the flow led to sliding between the sheets with this slightly tipsy siren. As he stared at her flushed cheeks, he wondered if a bourbon buzz would make it easier for her to have multiple orgasms or if that was just wishful thinking.

"And I thought *I* was full of myself?" She shook her head, her sleek blond hair sticking close to her scalp as if it had been too well trained to do otherwise. "You're one big walking, talking ego."

So maybe he couldn't honestly deny that charge. Still, he needed to make up for lost ground before he chased her away for good. "Sorry. Guess I wasn't thinking straight with all that—" his eyes jumped down her body without his permission, taking in her hips, lingering on her breasts "—sensory overload to contend with."

He could have been either sitting in a nice, air-conditioned bar with her right now or burning up the sheets and finding out firsthand how aggressive Lainie Reynolds would be in bed. Instead, he had pissed her off because he couldn't keep his thoughts to himself for more than five seconds at a time.

Well done, jackass.

"You're right."

What?

"You're kidding." He felt his eyes go wide. Since when was he right about anything when it came to women? He'd been screwing up in one form or another since college when he told Patti Lee Watkins he couldn't go to a party because he needed to practice his slap shot. Could he help it if he was a really honest guy? He'd remained a slave to hockey even though eventually he'd gotten laid despite himself, but right up until his last girlfriend dumped him, he'd continued to be oblivious about what women wanted to hear.

"I wasn't thinking straight, either. Partly because of the bourbon, partly because of the hormones in over-drive. And if I'm not thinking clearly, why should I expect you to?"

She nodded toward the street, obviously ready to continue their hike and not even bothering to pout at him. Damn but she was mature. He hoped he could keep pace with this woman.

"You sure you don't need a drink before we go?" He wanted to make up for being a heel. And she'd wanted a nightcap. Every woman's code name for sex, right? Still, maybe she was thirsty. "Let me get you something."

Before she could refuse, Nico scouted Ocean Drive for possibilities and found a churro stand, a Greek restaurant and—thankfully—an ice-cream vendor pushing a silver insulated freezer cart. "You can take ice cream on the road. Name your flavor, Lainie. It's on me."

Her steps slowed, her eyes, which had been mildly glazed before, now starting to clear as they locked on the ice-cream source. "I suppose I could be swayed with the promise of sweets. How about an Italian ice instead? Raspberry, I think.''

''Way to go out on a limb there and be decadent. Do you ever indulge yourself completely?'' Thankful he could do something to smooth things out between them, Nico ordered a triple scoop of chocolate pecan for himself along with her flavored ice. He handed her a stack of napkins and her wooden spoon while they waited.

Shrugging, she unwrapped the wooden stick that served as a utensil. ''My job is all about image. When I was an attorney, the best way to attract clients was to be the consummate professional. And now that I'm working with Club Paradise, the hotel is a reflection of me. I make an effort to always keep it together, although you've seen firsthand today that I'm not always successful.''

So she'd sipped some bourbon on the day her husband was held without bail. Big deal. Didn't she ever indulge in ice cream? In hot sweaty sex just for the sake of the thrill?

They walked down the street in the evening heat, the neon lights from the signs playing off the pastel-colored buildings to create a perpetual turquoise-and-pink glow. Lainie dug into her ice with her flat stick, the effects of the bourbon seeming to lessen as they walked and ate.

Nico couldn't decide if that was good or bad for him. He polished off his cone within a few blocks, long before she nibbled down the so-called treat she'd ordered.

''I believe Giselle mentioned something to me before she left about one of her brothers stopping by the club to check on the kitchens for her while she's away. Would that be you or one of her other siblings?"

"That would be me." His arm slipped around her as a crowd of rowdy, college-age guys piled out of a bar nearby.

She raised a curious eyebrow but didn't say anything. Yeah, that feel-good bourbon haze was definitely fading.

"Sorry. It's a guy thing." His arm slid away from her only through great willpower. "Automatic reflex."

Nodding, she tossed the paper cup and the stick from her ice in a trash can. "It's okay. But I was thinking maybe we'd better forget today ever happened once we get back to the hotel."

"Impossible."

"Excuse me?" Her tone assured him she hadn't been refused many times in her life.

"I couldn't forget today if you bribed me with an NHL contract. I'm attracted as hell to you, in case you haven't guessed already, and a guy just doesn't go home and forget about that."

"Nico, I'm flattered, but let me assure you I'm in no position to act on any kind of attraction right now." She squeezed her temples with her fingers as if the hangover headache was already setting in. "Not that I'm saying the attraction is two-way or anything."

God forbid.

"What's wrong with your position?" He enjoyed the view as he watched her strut down the street with her linen skirt still remarkably wrinkle free and her suit jacket folded neatly over her arm. "It looks damn good from where I'm standing."

She couldn't give him the brush-off now. Her siren's body had been melting in his arms half an hour ago, damn it. He'd been watching her for weeks and he was already halfway to obsessed. One thing was certain, if Lainie didn't like her current position, he had at least ten others in mind that would definitely please her.

LAINIE WAS NOT PLEASED.

Ever since she'd perfected her cool, dismissive look in law school, she'd been able to keep men at arm's length with no trouble. Men simply didn't chase her. Even in the case of her husband, she'd been the one to pursue him. Why wasn't Nico taking the very specific hints?

"Look, I'm sure you're used to women falling all over you with your jock appeal and your superstar status and all that." Could she help it if just a touch of sarcasm crept into her words? "But I've got a hotel to run and a bitter divorce still weighing me down like a Mack truck around my neck. I'm just trying to be honest with you about what you can expect from me."

"Which I'm rapidly realizing is nothing, according to you." His voice hummed a bit too close to her ear as they edged past a crowd gathering outside the velvet ropes of a new nightclub Lainie had been meaning to check out.

A shiver tripped through her at his nearness. She couldn't deny a little thrill at the way he maneuvered her through the milling people. His protective arm around her now and then might be a tad chauvinistic, but it left her no doubt he'd be quick to make sure nobody messed with her. Her shiver was an unusual sensation for a woman long accustomed to watching out for herself.

Still, she couldn't afford to get tied up in knots by a man again. Not now. Maybe not ever. Her divorce from Robert had ripped her raw and then turned her inside out. But since she had no intention of discussing the scarred state of her heart with Nico, she settled for counting down the more obvious, logical reasons that they would be all wrong together.

"For starters, did I mention how devastating it was to have your sister pull out as executive chef here last month? Don't get me wrong, I'm thrilled she's happy, but you have to see how difficult it's been filling her shoes." Giselle's contribution to the resort had been bigger than Lainie realized, and although Nico's sister maintained ownership of the controlling shares, she left a hell of a void in her place.

One that the new chef hadn't come close to filling, but Lainie was crossing her fingers the woman learned quickly.

When Nico didn't respond right away, she hurried on. "And did you know we've got a film crew coming to town to shoot a movie at Club Paradise?"

"What movie?"

"The press release called it a sexy action-adventure drama, if that tells you anything. Didn't Giselle tell you—Crap."

"What?"

"I forgot to tell Giselle about it. I thought maybe Summer or Brianne would tell her. It was Brianne's industry contacts that led to the club being used as a filming location. Did you know she used to be a director in New York before she invested in the resort and took over security?" Lainie hoped maybe if she threw out enough smoke-and-mirrors conversation, Nico would forget about her dictate that they go separate ways when they reached the hotel. She was feeling a little less weak-kneed now that she'd had something to eat, but she still had enough bourbon chugging through her system not to trust herself to make rational arguments tonight.

"Giselle told me. Not about the movie, but about Brianne having worked in film." He spoke absently, taking out the Hacky Sack that he toyed with like a lucky charm. Tossing the beanbag up in the air as he walked, he caught it three times in quick succession and then jammed it back in his pocket. "Having the movie filmed here—that's huge. Did you happen to catch the name of it?"

"It's called *Diva's Last Dance*. You see why I'm up to my eyeballs right now? We're down a partner and we've got to be more impressive than ever. I just think it would be easier if we—"

"You're not down a partner." He gestured to something up the street. "The resort is within view now. You think you'll be okay the rest of the way?"

She nodded, no longer tired thanks to his intriguing and potentially worrisome comment. "What do you mean we're not down a partner? Your sister has practically turned into Ms. Peace Corps now that she's overseas, and she's so damn starry-eyed in love I'd be surprised if she ever comes back to the club." Did he know something she didn't know?

They passed a group of drag queens dishing and primping in front of their compacts on the next street corner. The crowd of oversize men dressed in sexy dresses openly ogled Nico with whistles and catcalls. He made them all squeal by blowing them a kiss.

Lainie nearly commented on his obvious comfort with the locals until she realized he might be pulling his own version of conversational smoke and mirrors.

Before she could get back on track, he continued.

"I've read about this movie. It's a hot psychological drama where the heroine goes undercover to track a killer and ends up confronting the ghosts of her own past. Bram Hawthorne—the guy who's supposed to be the next Tom Cruise—is in it."

"Do I look like I'm lacking a pulse? Of course I know who Bram Hawthorne is. I didn't recognize the female lead's name though."

"Rosaria Graham. And trust me, guys know who she is."

"Oh really?" She didn't like Rosaria already. Not that she cared who Nico Cesare spent his time drooling over.

"I've read a few things about the movie, I just didn't know that some of it was being shot in Miami. But I heard the first actress quit because the script called for really graphic love scenes, so they called in Rosaria who has done a couple of mild adult films." He cleared his throat. "Or so I've heard."

A vision of Nico watching adult films flashed through her brain, followed quickly by an image of her watching with him. She'd never felt secure enough with any man to investigate the potential sensual possibilities of that kind of erotica, and not in a million years would she have ever gone out on a quest to explore that cinematic genre on her own. But the idea of watching with Nico....

Her breath caught in her throat as she remembered she had no business thinking about sex with this man. Scavenging up some righteous indignation—a far safer response—she sent him a level look.

"Are you telling me I'm hosting a porno flick on a four-star property?" Because no matter how much of a sex goddess this Rosaria person might be, Lainie would scream breach of contract so fast it would give those film executives whiplash if they tarnished the upscale image of her resort.

"Of course not. And some insiders are claiming that hiring her was all a publicity stunt anyway." He slowed his step as they reached Club Paradise, their long trek down South Beach finally at an end. "But obviously the producers want to get across a high steam level with this film."

"Okay, Roger Ebert. Care to tell me how you know all this about a movie that hasn't even been made yet?" Relieved to be back on familiar terrain, she stepped closer to the cover of a decorative palm tree near the Ocean Drive entrance of the resort.

Pride filled her to see the number of cars coming and going past the front doors, especially for a Monday. The Moulin Rouge Lounge was closed tonight, but the block still buzzed with activity.

"Giselle must have had a copy of *People* magazine lying around somewhere. During the hockey off-season, I tend to kick back a little bit. Read for entertainment." He withdrew his hand from his pocket to wrap it about her wrist, drawing her around the corner of the stucco building to the side of the Mediterranean-inspired hotel. His touch melted right through her skin, the warmth of his palm doing delicious things to her insides.

Lainie could hardly object to the move since she thought all along they shouldn't be seen together. Too complicated. "Well, regardless of where you found out all this, I appreciate you sharing it with me."

"No problem. But now I'll admit you've got me curious." He loomed closer suddenly, although Lainie hadn't seen him take any actual steps toward her. "You think you can handle all that steam under your roof day after day?''

He was so close she could feel the heat rise off his body. Memories of being pressed up against him sent waves of delicious awareness skating over her skin. She took a breath, steeling herself to give him the brush-off she desperately needed to impart.

''Anyone ever tell you that you have a hell of a lot of nerve?'' She congratulated herself that at least it hadn't come out of her mouth as a breathy rasp.

Take that, hormones.

''Nerve is an essential component of being a good goalie. I can't afford to let anything get past me, even if that means throwing myself in the path of speeding objects.'' He didn't touch her, but she thought she caught a hint of the bourbon on his breath.

Would he taste like that strong brew, or would his mouth be more reminiscent of chocolate ice cream? Neither possibility scared her off. If anything, her own mouth watered.

''I'm not a speeding object.'' She'd meant to deliver the words with a bit more disdain. Instead, she spoke by rote with no feeling behind the sentiment, like a woman in the throes of a sensual trance.

''Nevertheless, I'm not going to let you slide on by.'' His mouth descended to hers while she stood paralyzed by her own surprise.

Her own want.

But as his lips coaxed hers apart, the slick heat of his tongue sliding inside her mouth chased away the dazed sensation. Her hands gravitated to his chest, tracing over the wall of muscle she'd been longing to feel for hours. He cradled her chin in his palm, tilting her head to the angle that pleased him most, and by doing so, pleasing her to no end.

The lure of that kiss made her lean into him, her breasts already aching for contact. Her purse shifted on her shoulder, her linen jacket bunching up where she'd laid it across the leather bag.

The wrinkles, the discomfort of her heavy purse, none of it mattered. She only cared about that sizzling point of contact where their tongues tangled and their tastes blended.

Definitely chocolate ice cream. The sweetness of Nico Cesare's kiss belied all his nervy words and his earlier bold assumption that she wanted to crawl into bed with him. For this moment at least, his arrogance took a back seat to the skillful lash of his tongue and the delicate way he wove one hand through her hair, sifting the strands between his fingers while he kissed her as if he had all the time in the world.

She could have gone on forever, having long forgotten what made her want to protest this decadent mating of the mouths. But at that moment, a chorus of shrill screams went up in front of the hotel.

"It's Bram Hawthorne!"

More shrieks. Feet pounded the pavement all around them as if a stampede of buffalo in high heels had come gunning for Club Paradise.

Lainie and Nico broke apart, breathing heavy, clothes askew. She saw her own confused desire mirrored in his dark gaze for a fraction of a second before a herd of spandex-clad females buzzed past them at hyperspeed.

"Please don't let this be happening." Lainie hadn't expected the movie talent for another week or she never would have left the resort today. "Did they really just say what I think they said?"

The screams continued at a deafening pitch out front. No wonder it felt as if eyes were trained this way. Apparently they had been—just not on her. And it would only get worse once shooting began.

Nico stepped back a few feet, just far enough to give him a visual on the front entrance.

"Well?" Lainie tucked her shirt more firmly into her skirt and slipped into her jacket, her pulse still dancing a hip-hop beat through her veins.

Nico lifted a lone strand of mussed hair out of her eyes, his touch so gentle it gave her the same weak-kneed feeling as the bourbon, only better.

"I'd say either that kiss has me seeing stars or else your lead actor has arrived."

4

NICO HADN'T EXPECTED the look of mild horror on Lainie's face. It appeared for only an instant, a split second of blood draining from her cheeks while her eyes widened. Then she shook herself, and as if by the mere force of her formidable will, she drew herself up to her full height, threw her shoulders back and marched into the fray with complete authority.

Leaving Nico rushing to keep up, his senses still scrambled by her kiss. How was it possible that such a hard-as-nails woman could turn so soft in his arms?

He jogged the few steps to catch her on the walkway alongside the hotel, unwilling to let her be jostled and elbowed by a bunch of screaming fans. In his time as an NHL star, he'd seen his fair share of overzealous followers getting pretty out of hand. He couldn't even imagine what it must be like for a Hollywood icon of Bram Hawthorne's level of fame.

Like it or not, Lainie would have to suffer Nico's presence today. So what if she had insisted they part company once they got back to the resort? Club Paradise was in an uproar that could easily turn dangerous without the proper security in place.

As they rounded the corner to the front of the property, he could make out the Bram Hawthorne entourage by the concentration of popping flashbulbs. Hordes of howling women and even a few men swarmed around a center point Nico couldn't quite distinguish.

The poor bastard in the middle must be getting eaten alive by this rabid crowd. Lainie and Nico paused as they neared the mob.

"You need to hire more protection for the golden boy over there if you expect him to survive the filming." Nico studied the throng, searching for possible entry points to give the Hawthorne entourage a hand when he noticed Lainie's feet already in motion.

Right toward the vortex of the upheaval.

He double-timed to reach her, skirting between a few sensible fans hanging back from the mad whirlwind. Prying Lainie from her position between two teenage girls wearing T-shirts from Bram's last movie, Nico hauled her back out of the danger zone.

"What are you doing?" Shouting over top of the earsplitting screams of the fans, she glared at him with a look that would no doubt send her employees running for cover. "I've got a five-alarm fire to put out here. I don't have time to indulge any misguided attempts at chivalry."

"This isn't a matter of chivalry. Those women will tear you to shreds if you try to keep them from the object of their affection." In fact, he already spied a catfight breaking out among the ranks. "Where the hell is Brianne and all her security cameras?"

"I thought I caught a glimpse of red hair over that way." She pointed into the middle of the crowd as mayhem exploded on her sidewalk. "But she wasn't prepared for this yet and it's obvious she needs help. I'm going in there whether you like it or not. If you want to be of some assistance, you are welcome to come with me, but this is my hotel and you damn well better remember who's in charge here.''

This time, he was ready for her when she ducked into the throng. If his stint as a goalie had taught him anything, it was how to anticipate an opponent's moves.

"Then I'm damn well right behind you." And what a fine designer-clad behind it was.

AN HOUR LATER, Lainie still couldn't shake the determined company of Nico Cesare.

They'd intercepted Bram Hawthorne and had just finished helping smuggle him into the hotel. Thankfully, they'd managed to do so without losing the actor's shirt or his limbs despite the urgent tugging of relentless fans. With Bram and his personal crew of assistants already on their way up to their private suites, Lainie headed toward the main desk only to realize the rapid click of her footsteps was echoed by the quiet thump of worn leather loafers behind her.

She whirled around to face him, only to be taken aback all over again by how his long, muscular body and wickedly dark eyes made her pulse flutter. Even celebrated actor Bram Hawthorne's good looks took a back seat to this man's raw masculinity. At least in Lainie's opinion, which she realized might have been influenced by the most electrifying kiss of her whole life.

Gathering her wits, she knew the sooner she sent away big, gorgeous male distractions the better off she'd be. Her judgment in men had a hideous track record. No, her judgment in men didn't just have a record. It had a rap sheet.

"I appreciate your help with our new guest." She

smiled tightly, wishing she had never picked up a bottle of bourbon tonight. Her head throbbed with the stress of the day. "But I can take things from here."

She could already hear shouts for her attention from the registration desk. She had a thousand other things she needed to take care of before bed tonight, and none of them involved Nico.

"Why don't I stick around and see how things are going in the kitchen? Giselle asked me to make sure the new chef—"

He was cut off by the arrival of her big, burly concierge, an endlessly tall Cuban man with heavy horn-rimmed glasses and an accent to die for when he wasn't shouting over top of people.

"Ms. Reynolds!"

Even Nico backed up a step at the man's raised voice, which wasn't loud as much as very well projected.

Still, she didn't appreciate being interrupted. Especially when she was just about to explain to her sexy-as-sin companion why they couldn't work elbow to elbow like this.

She quirked an eyebrow in Dante Alvaro's direction, not trusting herself to speak. Rumor had it she'd scared off a few of the employees at Club Paradise in their first year of business, and while she didn't think rock-solid Dante would be easily intimidated, she didn't wish to blow her stack in such a public forum.

"Sorry for interrupting you, Lainie." His sour expression didn't look in the least sorry. Dante was usually a very charming man, dazzling the guests with his well-connected sleight of hand as he provided primo tickets and dinner reservations. Today, however, he looked positively grim. "But I knew you'd want to be informed immediately that the new chef quit an hour ago.''

No. No. *Nooo.*

Lainie closed her eyes, fending off a mixture of stress headache, hangover and dangerous levels of frustration threatening to explode. Her well-run hotel was suddenly splitting at the seams, making her feel like an amateur. God, she hated that.

Nico cleared his throat, edging his way into the conversation with his broad shoulders and his cute butt that should have left an hour ago. ''You can hire someone temporary in the morning while you conduct a new search, right? You must have résumés still on file after hiring this woman.''

''We have Hollywood royalty in the hotel. They're probably already phoning in room-service orders for green M&M's only and organically grown vegetables prepared according to their latest diet specifications. I don't think even Giselle would have been ready to cook according to the Sugar Busters plan, so I'm damn sure that some culinary temp worker isn't going to have a clue how to handle all the specialty orders.''

If she was hoping Dante would contradict her with some good news, her hopes were dashed when he began shaking his dark, bald head. ''We already had over fifty special orders for breakfast tomorrow when I left the kitchen an hour ago.''

Exasperation draining her of ideas, Lainie peered around the lobby and noticed more people who were obviously Californians crowding the reception area. They were easy to spot with their neat manicures and tans that were probably misted onto their perfect bodies. Cell phones were already ringing in cheerful time like an AT&T symphony.

"I thought these people weren't supposed to arrive for another three days." She would have had security in place by then. And she most definitely wouldn't have shown up on site with a few shots of bourbon muddling her brain and a sexy hockey player muddling her hormones.

Dante's deep brown eyes darted around the busy lobby, exchanging some unspoken message with his assistant currently manning the concierge's desk. "There was a hurricane in the Texas gulf that upset the location shooting schedule so they decided to visit Club Paradise early."

"You realize I'm so screwed?" For once she had no idea what to do, no clue who to call to straighten out this mess. This should all have been Giselle's department, damn it. She might have resigned her position as executive chef to pursue true love, but she still maintained an active share in the ownership of the resort. "We need to contact Giselle."

"Wait." Nico's voice halted her in her scramble for her cell phone.

Could the man be any more presumptuous, insinuating himself into her crisis?

"Nico, I really need to take care of this now." She felt Dante's keen gaze on her and knew if she didn't handle this carefully, the news of her odd friendship with Nico Cesare would be whispered all over the hotel.

"I agree." Nico nodded slowly, as if he'd just reached a grave decision. "But Giselle has been unreachable for nearly two days so she must be in some really godforsaken country at the moment."

So much for her great plan. She banged the cell phone slowly against her forehead, willing a solution to flash into her empty brain while Dante excused himself to get back to his desk.

"I know what we can do." Nico slid the phone out of her hand between forehead thunks.

We? Still, she couldn't afford to waste time arguing while her business reputation teetered on the brink of disaster.

"And that is?" She didn't care where the ideas came from as long as they came.

"I'll cook." He announced it with so much authority, a stranger to the resort would almost believe he had the decision-making power here.

Arrogant man.

"What do you mean you'll cook?" Was he insane? "You're not even a chef."

"Where do you think Giselle got all her best recipes?"

"Gee, I don't know." She rolled her eyes. "Culinary school, maybe? It would make sense since she's a chef and you're a hockey coach." After yanking her phone out of his hands, she stuffed it back in her purse. She would speed dial Brianne and Summer for an emergency conference call in a minute, but first she needed to send Nico back home where he wouldn't make ridiculous suggestions about how to run her business.

Where he wouldn't be a constant reminder that she'd let her hair down with a man for the first time in forever, and she was already paying the price for her carelessness.

"And I suppose *you're* going to do the cooking for all the eccentric eaters on your property tonight?" He looked her up and down as if he could see every one of the flaws she kept carefully hidden.

An illusion, damn it.

"Is that even legal?" Not that she was actually considering allowing Nico into the kitchen. Was she?

"Maybe. Probably. You can call me a guest chef specializing in ethnic cuisine if the health department cares about my qualifications."

"Ethnic cuisine?"

"Nobody makes Italian food like a Cesare." His chest puffed up with pride. "You think I'm kidding about Giselle learning all her best recipes from me? Besides, I told Giselle I'd check in at the hotel while she was gone to make sure her investment in the business is protected. She might be overseas, but she's still a partner. The Cesares have a vested interest in the smooth operation of this place."

Lainie glanced around the hotel lobby, seeing twenty other places she needed to be right now. The chef disaster couldn't have come at a worse time. What choice did she have besides accepting Nico's offer? At least until she came up with a better solution.

She'd simply agree to let Nico and his cute butt stick around Club Paradise a little longer. And if she couldn't stand the heat, all she had to do was stay away from the kitchen.

"Fine." She thrust out her hand to seal the deal. "I appreciate the help until I can make other arrangements tomorrow."

He enveloped her palm in his, his touch too gentle and too deliberate to qualify as a handshake. She shivered with awareness and hoped he didn't notice.

He smiled, that arrogant grin of his telling her he didn't miss a thing. "Agreed."

Extricating herself from that tempting touch, Lainie willed herself to cool down as she walked away. But when a male chuckle echoed in her ears, she had the feeling it didn't matter how much distance she put between her and the kitchen.

Things were already beginning to heat up.

"THIS MOVIE'S ALL ABOUT SEX, steam and sizzle," Hollywood A-lister Bram Hawthorne declared around a mouthful of scrambled eggs the next morning as he sat across the table from Nico in the back of the Club Paradise kitchen. "I don't know if it will have any kind of critical success, but I think moviegoers are going to love it."

Nico wolfed down his own plate of food in the lull between the insane breakfast hours and the upcoming lunch crowd. He'd cooked his butt off all morning—everything from dry wheat and basic eggs over easy to complicated omelets and breakfast soufflé. Thankfully, a local vendor had been delivering plenty of pastries ever since Giselle left, so he'd avoided that headache. But still, Nico had never worked so hard in his life. Even a full day of practice defending rapid-fire, one-on-one breakaway shots had been a walk in the park compared to cooking for two hundred guests.

And when it was all over, Bram Hawthorne's manager had come sneaking in the back door with the movie's most bankable talent so the star could eat his breakfast in peace. Nico might have been more starstruck if he hadn't been so exhausted.

The discussion of sex and steam caught his attention, however. Especially since his cooking had been impaired by thoughts of sex and steam with Lainie Reynolds.

"From what I've heard about the movie, it sounds like it's got story to spare, too. Critics seem more tol-

erant of sex and sizzle if there's some substance to back
it up.'' Nico had been a closet movie buff since forever.
The cinema had been the only place for real escape
after he'd lost his mom as a kid, and then his dad as a
teenager. Something about a darkened theater gave you
the illusion of being able to walk away from your own
hurts and step straight into the fantasy world on screen.

Come to think of it, maybe that was part of his ob-
session with Lainie. She was a fantasy. A tough-as-
nails businesswoman who posed an enticing challenge
but would never be interested in the long haul. And
after his experience with Ashley, that sounded just right
to him.

''That'd be a nice bonus.'' Bram grinned and a hint
of his Mississippi accent drawled through his words.
He couldn't be any older than twenty-five, but he'd
been a Hollywood phenomenon since a walk-on appearance as a flamboyant waiter in a Harrison Ford
flick. ''But I've found out firsthand that what the critics
say don't figure into your paycheck. Actors get paid
for how many seats they fill at the theater—end of
story.''

Nico nodded, a little surprised at the Machiavellian
thinking in a twenty-five-year-old, but who was he to
judge? Bram seemed nice enough. He had the Joe
Movie Star grin going with fifty-thousand megawhite
teeth, but he was lucky if he hit six feet in boots. Spiky
brown hair and gray eyes made up for a lot with
women, apparently. But the guy had to be pretty damn
down-to-earth to break bread in the kitchen with a
sweaty athlete posing as a cook.

''More coffee?'' Yet another waitress appeared to
fill their cups, the third new face at their table since
they'd sat down.

This one was blond and blue-eyed and way too innocent looking. She was the antithesis of Lainie Reynolds in every way but the hair color. Where Lainie was sleek and sophisticated, this woman nearly bubbled over with energy and too much enthusiasm.

Or maybe that was only when she waved a coffeepot under a superstar's nose.

"None for me, thanks." Bram had been polite to all the waitresses, doling out grins every time he'd been interrupted.

Nico could think of too many hockey stars who couldn't be bothered to be nice to anyone in the food-service industry unless they were out to...get laid.

His gaze tracked back to Bram. Had the guy been lining up after-hours entertainment all this time?

"Then is there anything else I can get for you?" The fluffy-haired waitress leaned forward, her bountiful breasts now prominently displayed.

Shoving his last bite of eggs in his mouth, Nico knew when he was being a third wheel. He scraped his chair backward across the ceramic tiles when a sharp feminine voice pierced the din of kitchen sounds.

"Excuse me, miss, may I ask what you think you're doing in my hotel?" Lainie cruised to a stop beside the table, belatedly taking in her famous guest's presence. "If I'm not mistaken, you're no longer employed here."

Nico noticed her already perfect posture straighten by a few more taut degrees. If he hadn't seen her barefoot and sipping homemade Kentucky brew with his own eyes yesterday, he never would have thought her capable of loosening up an inch. She wore a navy suit with some sort of black-lace camisole thing underneath and a strand of fat pearls around her neck. He squinted

hard to get a better view of the black-lace thing, but
with her jacket buttoned, he could only make out about
two square inches. Just enough to make him undress
her shamelessly with his eyes while she spoke to the
red-faced waitress.

"My girlfriend who works in the coffee shop has a
room here this week," the younger woman shot back.
"We're trying out as extras for the movie." She
hooked her thumb in the pocket of her jeans and cast
a sly smile in Bram's direction. "I'm Daisy Stephenson, by the way."

"But what are you doing *here,* in the kitchen, which
you know perfectly well is an employees-only area?"
Lainie arched her eyebrow, her gaze never wavering
from the waitress who perhaps wasn't a waitress, after
all. In fact, she didn't even have a uniform on, just a
coffeepot in her hand.

Bram cleared his throat. "Sorry to have descended
on you like this, ma'am." He reached into his wallet
and laid way too much money on the table for the eggs
Nico had made him. "It's my fault for bringing out-
siders into the kitchen, but I had my manager check
with your chef and he seemed to think it would be
okay."

Nico couldn't believe the guy was throwing him in
the fire on this one. He didn't remember okaying the
presence of a pseudowaitress. But before he could say
yea or nay on the cock-and-bull story, Lainie was already relenting.

"Of course it's not a problem, Mr. Hawthorne." She
doled out a very pleasant expression to smooth things
over, but Nico noted she still didn't smile. Not really.
Her stretching of the lips was Mona Lisa-esque at best.
"I hear you're starting filming already today, so we'll

just be out of your way.'' She stepped away from the table, presumably to give Nico room to rise and join her. ''Don't hesitate to let me know if there's anything I can do to make your visit more comfortable.''

Nico didn't rise just yet, watching the Hollywood superstud across the table for any signs of hitting on Lainie. There'd damn well be arsenic in the eggs tomorrow if his eyes roamed anywhere near that black-lace job she wore.

Lucky for him, Bram nodded with squeaky-clean good manners. ''Will do. I appreciate that, ma'am.''

Smart kid.

Nico rose to his feet, balancing every last dish on his forearms as he made his way over to the sterilizing sinks. He was in the process of turning over the plates to the dishwasher when he realized the click-click of Lainie's high heels hadn't followed him.

Jealousy niggled as he envisioned Mr. Hollywood Charm laying it on thick behind Nico's back. His jaw flexed, hands clenched in anticipation.

Yet when he turned, he spied Lainie in heated conversation—not with Joe Movie Star, but with the wanna-be movie extra.

IF HIS TIME HAD BEEN HIS OWN, Bram Hawthorne could have spent another hour in the Club Paradise kitchen shooting the breeze with hockey legend Nico Cesare and making eyes at the stacked waitress with sweet blue eyes. Bram hadn't enjoyed such a normal, peaceful meal since he'd started work on *Diva's Last Dance* two months ago. There were plenty of advantages to being the Hollywood star on the rise, but eating a meal in peace wasn't one of them.

He looked back into the kitchen one more time before he plowed through the swinging doors to seek out his new shooting location. The blond waitress with the sex-goddess body—Daisy—looked as if she was being chewed out by the hotel manager or owner or whoever this Lainie Reynolds person was supposed to be. The woman in the high-class suit must have been a studio executive in another life.

Damn, but he should have just corralled the flirty blonde under his arm and taken her to the filming with him so he could have spared her an ass chewing.

The thought inevitably pulled his eyes southward to check out the ass in question. So fine. Tight and succulent and so much better than Hollywood female butts, which fell into two categories—anemic or iron-clad.

He'd stake his considerable paycheck that her breasts were the real deal, too. He'd seen enough silicone up close and personal to be able to appreciate the soft sway of God-given twins.

Yes, ma'am, he would make time for Daisy in his future.

But right now he had a scene to shoot. Allowing the swinging door to fall shut on the scene in the kitchen, he checked his watch and then sprinted up a set of emergency stairs, which were always less populated than the elevator. He'd promised his all-business costar that he'd be on the set early to run through their actions and get a feel for the environment.

For all her sex-queen reputation, Rosaria Graham was as hard-nosed and driven as they came. Silicone from head to toe, the woman probably had a synthetic heart, too. The only time she mustered up any warmth of personality was when the director or one of the studio reps happened by the set.

As for warming up to her fellow actors—forget it. Taking the stairs two at a time, Bram acknowledged Rosaria's only form of interaction with him so far had been to critique his performance and tell him what he should be doing differently. Not that she gave a rat's butt about seeing him succeed. She just figured that the better he acted, the bigger their box-office sales would be and the more parts she'd be offered.

Little did Rosaria know Bram had his own reasons for making every performance the best he could. Reasons that went a hell of a lot deeper than earning enough cash to finance more silicone and a new Rolls. Shoving aside thoughts of his sister and the unidentified disease she battled every day while he climbed the ladder to stardom, Bram vowed this movie wouldn't be any different. He'd cash in with *Diva's Last Dance* even if Rosaria was proving to be a first-class snot.

Reaching the floor where they'd be shooting today's scene, Bram plowed through the heavy steel door with both arms, winging the weighted barrier so hard it creaked on its hinges. And nearly slamming into a big, beefy guy covered in tattoos who looked downright pissed at the close encounter.

Until the scowling man recognized him. Bram signed an autograph while the towering brute showed off his favorite body art—a toss-up between the mermaid on his right shoulder and the surfboard on his left. Bram smiled and nodded and hurried away, reminding himself to focus on his upcoming performance.

And thankfully, Daisy the waitress was going to be the new key to his motivation for his upcoming love scenes. All he'd have to do was envision Daisy in Rosaria's place and he'd be golden.

In fact, now that he thought about it, he had a good idea how he could be even more inspired. Nearing the Fun & Games Chamber, Bram tugged out his cell phone and put in a call to one of the film's gofers to request the best motivation of all.

He might not be able to act out this scene with the woman he'd been thinking about, but he sure as hell could arrange to have her there. Close enough to see. Close enough to fantasize about.

Whipping off a few instructions, Bram congratulated himself for his quick thinking. With the flirtatious Daisy standing by, he knew he'd be turning in one hell of a love scene because the secret of his success was that he possessed great imagination.

He just hoped he wouldn't have to imagine what Daisy tasted like for long. Sooner or later, he wanted the real deal all for himself.

THE URGE TO PULL A HANK of Daisy Stephenson's bottle-blonde shag cut rode Lainie so hard she thought it best to fist her hands behind her back.

"I don't care that Bram Hawthorne is allowed to enter the kitchen. You are not." Lainie had fired Daisy from her position as a cigarette girl in the resort's nightclub nine months ago after the woman had continually thrown herself at Brianne's boyfriend-turned-fiancé. Bad enough Daisy had foisted her attentions on an FBI agent who'd been investigating the club at the time, but she'd also frequently left her workstation to pursue her hormonal needs.

Lainie had no intention of letting the woman weasel her way into the resort to wreak havoc again. Especially not when Lainie's best PR chance of all time loomed within her reach.

Daisy fluffed her hair at her shoulder as she pursed bubblegum-colored lips. "You may have to rescind that dictate if I'm on the list of things Bram requests to make him more comfortable." She hitched up the narrow strap of her tank top, dragging her twenty-pound breasts upward with the motion.

Tart.

Lainie knew worse words to describe Daisy, but she didn't dare think them for fear they'd trip out of her lips. "Just as long as he doesn't request your presence in any employees-only areas, I'm sure you made it patently obvious he can have you anywhere he wants you."

Turning on her heel before she allowed Daisy to tick her off any further, Lainie nearly crashed right into Nico.

"Morning." He looked too damn good for a man who'd fielded a record number of room-service orders, according to her kitchen sources. A big white chef's apron covered part of his black slacks and a gray polo shirt. He smelled like the antibacterial soap the kitchen stocked by the gallon. Casting a sideways glance at Daisy as the woman blasted through the swinging doors and out of the kitchen, he raised an eyebrow. "I take it she's not a friend of yours."

"Don't even ask." She whipped a sheet of paper out of the leather binder she carried and waved it in front of him. The more barriers between her and Nico, the better. "The good news is I've got a few interviews lined up this afternoon for the executive chef position."

"Great. But what are the chances anybody's going to be able to start today?" He ripped open an industrial-size bag of pasta sitting next to him on the kitchen counter.

"I don't know. But Brianne suggested we tell all the candidates that part of the interview includes seeing how they handle the working environment, so we've got the next two meals covered." She continued to clutch the paper in front of her like a shield, even though Nico was maneuvering around the kitchen with slow, easy movements. "You're off the hook, Nico. Thanks for all the help, but we should be able to manage things from here."

And she should be able to find her equilibrium again just as soon as this magnetic male found the exit.

Nodding, Nico accepted the news with less enthusiasm than she would have expected. He untied his apron and ducked out of the garment before tossing it in a linen bin.

"That's great. But I don't know if I'm ready to leave quite yet."

Crap.

She told herself she was disappointed even as a ridiculous little surge of excitement tripped through her.

Crap times two. She could not afford to have her head turned by an arrogant ex-athlete with an overabundance of testosterone.

"Why not? Have you decided you've found your true calling in the restaurant business?" Being a wiseass might help her remember to keep him at arm's length. She hoped.

Nico stepped closer. Crowded her. "Actually, I was hoping I could talk you into a little steam, sex and sizzle."

5

NICO WAITED TO SEE THE SPARKS leap in Lainie's sea-green eyes the way they had yesterday right before they'd kissed. He was pushing his luck today with her, but her sleekly perfect exterior and her cool-as-you-please demeanor begged for riling. Tousling. And he wanted to be the man to derail all that smooth control.

He wanted the fantasy, damn it. A close encounter in the hotel kitchen would fill the bill nicely.

"Apparently your brain waves are misfiring this morning," she shot back, no sparks apparent in her gaze at all. "Because you seem to have just said something utterly ridiculous. Do you care to try that again?"

From the icicles dripping off her words, Nico guessed he was halfway home to riling her. His morning was improving by the minute.

"I asked if you wanted to share some steam, sex and sizzle with me." Just saying the word *sex* to Lainie made him hot as hell. "The scene from the movie that they're filming today is supposed to be the first sensual encounter between the hero and heroine. I thought you might want to go check it out with me."

Lainie took two deep breaths, the motion doing intriguing things to the black lace beneath her suit jacket. The paper she'd been holding between them had fallen to her side as if forgotten, giving him a much better view of her...outfit.

"They don't let just anybody show up on the set of a love scene." She busied herself with returning her paper to her leather binder. Straightening it. Adjusting the position of a silver pen clipped above a legal pad. "Apparently you haven't read Giselle's *People* magazine closely enough if you don't know that."

A new influx of kitchen staffers shoved through the swinging doors as lunchtime neared. Not ready for this conversation to end just yet, Nico gave Lainie a nudge toward the food-supply closet.

"Maybe that's true most of the time, but remember who they've got for a female lead on this picture."

"The porn queen?" She surprised him by stepping into the large pantry area without argument.

He crossed his fingers that maybe she enjoyed their topic of conversation as much as he did. "The adult actress. And the director told me over breakfast that she likes doing love scenes with an audience. It enhances her performance."

"The director told you this?" She sounded part skeptical and part…interested.

"Yeah. Right after he picked up his vegetable omelette made with imitation, cholesterol-free eggs. And right before he invited me to drop by the set this afternoon." He wondered if Club Paradise's diva-in-charge would be turned on by the movie preview. "What do you say? Will you go with me? The part they're filming today doesn't involve anything super-risqué. It's more a prelude to a love scene."

"How is it you've been helping out here for all of twelve hours and you've already had breakfast with the hottest man in Hollywood and secured an invite to a movie set?"

"It sure as hell wasn't the vegetable omelette." He

would have blown off the question but she looked serious as she rocked back on her heels in front of a shelfful of flour bags. "It probably has something to do with my sports career. Most hockey fans know who I am, even if I'm not on the ice anymore."

And while it was cool to be recognized, it really sucked not to be skating.

Her lips thinned, flattened. "I forgot you were famous in your own right."

"Is that a bad thing?" Stepping over a box of canned chicken broth, he inched closer, hoping nobody in the kitchen would need anything out of the pantry for a few more minutes.

"Your celebrity status is of no consequence to me. I've had quite enough notoriety lately, thanks to my ex." She shifted as he neared, as if she was making plans to bolt. "And thanks for the invitation to the filming, but I'd really better join Brianne to meet the first interviewee. They'll probably be arriving in the kitchen any minute."

Curving his hands around her upper arms, he held her in place. She sucked in a gasp but didn't tell him to back off. "Go with me."

"I just said—"

"How often are you going to have a chance to see a movie in production in your life? And it's set at your hotel. Shouldn't you be kissing up to all these film people with deep pockets and good connections anyway?"

He'd worry about making her stay longer once he convinced her to go in the first place. He had the feeling he'd need all the help he could get to make headway with this woman who'd been burned big-time by her ex. What could be better than to watch a love scene in progress? Maybe she'd be so inspired she'd unbutton that jacket of hers and give him a better glimpse at whatever she wore beneath.

As if she could guess his thoughts, her breathing went shallow and quick. He caught the scent of her, dark and exotic amid the smell of sterilizing dishwater wafting in from the kitchen.

"Maybe a few minutes would be okay." Her nod was almost imperceptible, as if she hadn't fully talked herself into agreeing. "I did want to offer to procure any necessary backdrops for their scenes if they need them."

It was his cue to slap himself on the back and accept victory graciously. He was ahead one-nothing with only minutes to go in the game. But all his years as a hockey goalie hadn't done much to teach him good defense.

To his way of thinking, the sooner he could score, the better.

Cornering her against the shelfful of flour, he bracketed her body with his arms as he braced himself up against the metal racks. "And who knows? Maybe today's scene will give you a few ideas."

"Really?" She was breathing every bit as fast as him as he leaned closer still.

"I thought maybe you'd enjoy a little more steam and sizzle." He was whispering the last few words by the time his mouth slanted over hers.

Voices sounded outside the door, the din of lunch prep already beginning. Nico knew this wasn't the time or place, but he had apparently forgotten to communicate as much to his lips.

Lainie tipped her head back, exposing her long neck

encircled by fat pearls, reminding him that she wore something really incredible under her suit.

His hand sought out the smooth column of her throat, skimming over the warm skin as he tasted her. Palm bumping over the negligible barrier of the pearls, he continued south to her collarbone, beneath her jacket.

Her heart galloped under his hand and she let out a small sigh. He was millimeters away from black lace when the slice of light from the kitchen widened into a bright band of obnoxious fluorescence.

Busted.

"And this is the food supply clos—" Brianne Wolcott, a statuesque redhead who co-owned Club Paradise, halted her narrative as she spotted them. "Whoops."

Nico swore he could feel every last one of Lainie's muscles tense. Tighten.

She didn't meet his eye as she hastened forward to make excuses and slip away from Brianne's kitchen tour with the chef candidate. But Nico didn't need to see her eyes to know he'd made a bad play decision late in the game. He'd gone for broke when he should have been playing conservatively.

Now Lainie was walking away, and every last twitch of her incredible hips seem to shout, "Game over."

SHE WAS *NOT* HYPERVENTILATING from Nico's kisses. Lainie sat in her office ten minutes later, assuring herself her inability to catch her breath could very well be stress-related, due to the million and one projects she needed to juggle today. Or it could be embarrassment because Brianne and the new chef applicant had walked in on her and Nico engaged in the most pulse-racing moment of her entire life.

Gripping the edges of her carved mahogany desk to keep herself steady, Lainie decided whatever had prompted the sudden attack of breathlessness, it was not the burning imprint of Nico's hand spanning her collarbone and down to the top of one aching breast.

Lainie had bolted from the kitchen under the pretense of a hotel emergency, but she'd heard Nico stay behind to introduce himself to the interviewee. Brianne could handle the chef candidate while Lainie got her head together. In fact, she needed to be better about delegating work now that the resort faced its biggest guest-service challenge yet. She should be actively freeing up time to schmooze the movie's location coordinator. To go catch snippets of the crew in action while they filmed...

Steam, sex and sizzle.

Damn it, she should be there this afternoon whether she went with Nico or not. So what if it felt like a naughty indulgence to watch an actor and actress fog the camera lens with Nico by her side? It was part of her job, and Lainie had never, ever shirked her responsibilities.

Allowing her head to fall to her marble-topped desk, she hoped if she closed her eyes for just a few seconds she would regain her equilibrium. Already her breathing had quieted.

The cool marble felt good against her heated forehead. She folded her arms beneath her to give her a better cushion, but as she rearranged her head on the desk, her elbow scraped across a piece of paper out of place.

Not a frequent occurrence for her since she normally kept her desk immaculately organized.

Shifting in her seat, she sat upright to retrieve the stray sheet and return it to its rightful place. Yet as her eyes roamed over the crisp linen stock she realized she'd never seen it before. Two lines of neat penmanship had been centered in the middle of the page.

Guess your chef quit at an inopportune time. I sure hope it's not the first of many troubles to come.

☺

The irreverent smiley face really irritated her. Why would someone leave such a smart-ass note on her desk?

A rap at her office door startled her.

"Come in." She straightened, stuffing the note in her binder.

The door opened and Nico stepped inside, his shoulders relaxed. His breathing perfectly normal, damn the man.

"Ready to go?" He shoved his hands in his pockets and peered around her workspace. "Great office."

She rather liked the combination of black, red and gold decor herself when she wasn't fuming over an anonymous stranger's snotty insolence. One wall of her workspace overflowed with black-and-white prints of Club Paradise throughout its renovation stages. Nico seemed to be studying the erotic theme rooms with special interest.

"Thank you." Standing, she put the note out of her mind. While those stark centered lines had read to her like a warning, they could also simply be taken as someone's dopey attempt to commiserate with her on a tough day.

Although it seemed even the dopiest of someones would at least sign their letter.

"I missed out on a lot of the earlier renovations because of hockey season." He bent to peer more closely at a photo she happened to know depicted the four owners conducting one of their early business meetings in an outdoor hot tub.

It had been fun in those first few months, but Lainie thought it was even more fun to be operating in the black with a growing profit margin.

She watched Nico move down the wall of photos, his gaze taking in the theme rooms from the Bordello Room to the Harem Suite. From the Vixen's Villa to the Pleasure Parthenon.

"Wow." He tugged at the collar of his gray polo shirt. "You've got some spicy digs here."

"Didn't Giselle ever take you on a tour of the theme rooms?" She just assumed he'd seen the whole hotel already.

"Honestly, I never liked the idea of my baby sister working in someplace so risqué so I didn't let her take me on the tour."

"Your baby sister who's what—twenty-five now? No wonder she took off for a new continent if that's how you treated her." She stood, her whole body too restless to be in such close quarters with Nico after they'd just been plastered together in a supply closet.

She would probably be better off with the camera crew watching a sexy love scene than standing all alone in her office with a man whose kisses made her toes curl.

"Bad decision by me. I know that now. My sister wasn't cut out for the convent, much as I may have hoped otherwise.'' He paused as she was sidling closer to the door. ''Is everything okay?''

''Perfect. I'm ready to go when you are.'' She forced herself to stand very still. In her days as a practicing attorney, her ability to stare a man down had won her more court cases than she could count, but her skills felt a bit rusty when she tried them out on Nico. He seemed more than ready to lock gazes with her.

''You seem a little jumpy.''

She sighed, frustrated. ''If you're expecting me to say I'm all aflutter because of one little kiss, I guarantee you're talking to the wrong woman.''

''Did you just refer to that kiss as *little?*''

''Okay, here we go.'' She rolled her eyes and reached for the doorknob. ''Male ego at work, I suppose. So sorry for the slip.''

Nico didn't shut the door and argue the point about the kiss, and if she were honest she'd have to admit maybe she was just a smidge disappointed about that.

Still, as they made their way down the hall toward the Fun & Games Chamber, she couldn't deny the shiver that tripped through her when he whispered in her ear.

''Remind me to move straight into the *big* kisses next time we find ourselves in a supply closet, okay?''

''You should be so lucky, Slick.'' Feeling marginally more in control now that she'd made it clear what happened between them had been no big deal, Lainie led them to the suite where the filming was scheduled to take place.

She'd stay ten minutes, tops. Just long enough to make nice with the location director and offer the hotel's services with anything the film crew might need. Then she and Nico could part company before her reawakened hormones got any ideas. Because no matter how hot their kisses, Lainie couldn't handle a relationship right now. Not even the simple, sexual kind that her hormones screamed she should share with Nico.

Men were a scary proposition in her experience. Before Brianne had gotten engaged to Aidan, she'd been stalked by a lunatic guitar player who'd been obsessed with her. Then there was Summer's old beau—the megatattooed former restaurant manager of Club Paradise who'd cheated on her before he left town with the rest of his cronies. He was a low-level operator in the Rat Pack group, but he was one of the few original members of the crew who'd managed to elude police since they could never get enough evidence to convict him of anything.

And then there'd been Lainie's personal experience, which only further proved that a girl couldn't be too careful when it came to men.

Her life currently operated in big, fat rebound mode. In fact, she was so deep in rebound territory she'd probably bounce if she weren't wearing spike heels at the moment.

No men. No relationships. And definitely no big kisses.

NICO DIDN'T KNOW WHAT he'd expected from Club Paradise's Fun & Games Chamber, but it sure as hell hadn't been this.

After one of the set assistants admitted them into the huge suite and ushered them to a viewing area taped off for guests, he tried not to gawk at the wide assortment of what he could only assume to be sex toys and possibly S and M contraptions. There was an inverted, gravity-defying table for hanging people upside down.

Only this didn't look like the one at his old gym. This was padded in well-oiled leather and included velvet handcuffs for complete immobilization.

Damn.

The room also featured a net suspended from the ceiling. A hammock maybe. Or a swing. He didn't have a clue. Was it somehow a turn-on to have sex while suspended? Sounded to him like a surefire way to fall on your ass. Did Ms. Sleek and Sophisticated Lainie Reynolds know what all these things were used for?

This was her hotel, after all.

He couldn't decide if he should be jealous or turned on by Lainie having explicit carnal knowledge about such a wide range of intimate accessories.

There were velvet shackles dripping from the ceiling at various intervals, so, in case you forgot to cuff your partner in the kitchenette, you could still find conveniently located restraints on your way to the bedroom. Or the bathroom. Or right in front of the plasma-screen TV. Pretty freaking convenient.

He also spotted an oversize birdcage that perhaps wasn't for birds, a piece of exercise equipment that probably wasn't used for exercise as he knew it and a glass case holding a see-through mannequin outfitted in full-out S and M garb. And it looked so damn complicated with all its metal rings and leather straps that he figured it was just as well there was a model in place or horny couples would be there all night trying to figure out what strap went where.

"So what do you think?" Lainie whispered as they settled on a pair of chrome bar stools someone had dragged over from the kitchen area. They were confined to the taped-off area with seven other people, but the only face Nico recognized a few feet away was Daisy, the fake waitress who'd caught Bram Hawthorne's eye earlier that day.

Apparently she'd wrangled an invitation to the filming, as well.

"I think you're running a damn kinky operation, lady." Maybe she could be persuaded to give him a personal guided tour of the erotic haven after the movie finished filming here. A tour *and* a demonstration. "Is it legal to have all this stuff in a hotel?"

"I assume so since this room is especially popular with several high-ranking city police officials. Though not at the same time of course." She hugged her leather binder closer to her chest as the camera crew wheeled around lights on dollies. "I meant what do you think of the sneak peek at the movie business?"

Who could absorb the drama of the movie business while surrounded by so much sex paraphernalia? Still, he tried to block out the erotic images that seemed to bombard him from every corner and focus on the small group of production and technical people debating how to stage the scene. Bram stood on the periphery of their conversation, offering occasional input.

The adult-film star, Rosaria, lounged across a leopard-print divan, her well-known breasts clad in a halter top that had as much substance as a cocktail napkin. Her red leather pants were skintight, which was a good thing because her total lack of hips would have made it difficult for jeans to remain on her body otherwise. She made notes on a piece of paper, rereading and occasionally crossing out what she'd written.

"I think it looks sort of highbrow and glamorous just because it's set in your hotel. Without the sex trappings as a backdrop, the actual movie-making equipment isn't all that impressive.'' He wanted to ask if she'd ever stayed in the Fun & Games Chamber, but thought better of it.

A light snapped off beside the small crowd of guest viewers as the director called last-minute instructions to the actors to just keep going and ride out the scene to see how it felt. The area where the action would be staged was illuminated as bright as Christmas while the rest of the room remained in darkness. The effect was similar to viewing a movie in the theater. Private, anonymous, engaging.

Nico resisted the urge to slide an arm around Lainie and draw her close while they settled in to watch the show.

DAISY STEPHENSON TRIED very hard to ignore her nemesis a few feet away as she concentrated on the latest object of her affections prowling the perimeter of the set inside the Fun & Games Chamber.

Bram.

Top-shelf, first-class Hollywood royalty, the man could be her ticket to bigger and better things. After all, how long could she stick around South Beach just to make Lainie Reynolds's life difficult? The men in Miami were beginning to bore her.

And not just because she'd already slept with her fair share. No, she simply didn't want to waste another Saturday night making small talk with some Brazilian polo player who barely spoke English or a French race-car driver who thought he was so much smarter than her just because she happened to enjoy discussing shopping more than fuel injection.

So sue her for being just a smidge on the materialistic side. When you grew up with nothing, you learned to appreciate every *something* that came your way.

And Bram Hawthorne…he was something.

His good-old-boy accent had charmed her from the moment he'd opened his mouth in the kitchen. Of course, in all honesty she probably would have chased him whether he'd charmed her or not, given that he was an honest-to-God movie star. But it sure made the chase more fun when she considered how genuinely nice he'd seemed.

Perhaps she just didn't travel in the right circles, but it had been her experience that there weren't very many nice people in the world. Everyone had an agenda. Shoot, she'd be the first to admit she had one. She even kept lots of little lists to be sure she was accomplishing tasks on the way to her big goals. Life was all about getting ahead.

"Daisy?" The Southern accent lingering over the syllables in her name jerked her attention back to the movie scene. The gray-eyed male who'd spoken made her heart beat faster.

Bram Hawthorne had called to her from his spot on the set near his incredibly gorgeous costar who looked as if she'd been poured out of the same mold as a Barbie doll.

Daisy waved to him in response, not sure what the etiquette would be for guests at the filming. She didn't want to get kicked out before this scene of Bram's even started. The scene he'd wanted her to see.

She got all tingly just thinking about it. He'd had one of his assistants track her down in the lobby to invite her to the taping. Surely that boded well for possibly hooking up later? A tryst with a superstar hadn't been on her list of ways to flaunt what she'd made of herself in front of her family before she left South Beach for good, but it would fill the bill. Not that she carried a grudge against her mom and dad for making her feel like the town slut when she'd gotten pregnant in high school by the first guy in her life who made her feel special.

After losing the baby in a miscarriage and losing the guy thanks to her dad's threats, Daisy had given up seeking family approval. If anything, she'd probably sought sex for sex's sake too many times since then just to assure herself she was in charge of her own life and could make her own decisions. But lately she'd realized that if she continued that pattern of behavior, she'd be every bit the town slut they'd long ago accused her of being. Rather than live up to the world's low expectations of her, she'd decided to ship out of South Beach in search of new beginnings.

But it couldn't hurt to chase a man for the sake of his bod this one last time. And if her mother turned green with envy that Daisy had finally struck gold in her man quest, that was just frosting on the cake.

Speaking of sweet treats, the cake in question wore a ripped T-shirt and jeans that looked as if he'd slept in them for three days. Jeans that also happened to showcase his package very nicely. Women all over the world would thank the costume designer.

As she daydreamed about what lay underneath those jeans of his, she realized he was headed her way even though the director had just said they were almost ready to start.

"Thanks for coming." He smiled at her as he neared the roped-off area where the guests stood. "Hope you don't mind me sending somebody else downstairs to look for you, but I wanted you to be here to see this."

Something in his voice sounded so sincere. So genuine. Maybe it was just because he was an actor and he was better at picking up women than most guys. Still, she couldn't help but smile back as she lowered her voice to bedroom volume. "Then I guess I'll be sure to keep my eyes on you."

"Bram?" The director called to him in a moment of supremely bad timing. Daisy could have sworn Bram had been about to say something nice. Maybe even flirt right back with her.

"Ready." He sounded so sure of himself as he nodded to the director, a short, androgynous-looking woman dressed all in black.

Daisy rocked back on her heels, ready to take in the show. Whatever was going to happen in his scene today, Bram obviously wanted her to see it.

She just hoped it wouldn't take long, because she had the feeling she wouldn't be able to get a good look at what she *really* wanted to see of his until later.

"CAN YOU SEE OKAY?" Nico whispered the words in Lainie's ear just so he could have an excuse to get closer to her. He breathed in her scent as the director shouted for everyone to take their places.

Lainie nodded, her attention on the shuffling of camera operators now, even though she'd been staring at Daisy the pseudowaitress just a few moments ago, steam almost visibly hissing from her ears.

Now the former Club Paradise employee seemed to settle in to watch her quarry. In fact, she'd just pulled a notepad from her shoulder bag and proceeded to scribble a few lines on a piece of paper. Nico briefly wondered if the wily female had a game plan for how to snag a superstar. He sure hoped Bram was more discriminating about his taste in groupies than Nico had been.

. But as Lainie's heady scent rode the scant space between them, Nico's thoughts drifted back to the scene. To Lainie.

They watched together as Rosaria Graham tossed her long black curls over her shoulder and settled into the divan. Whipping out a set of playing cards, she flipped them into a solitaire arrangement. Bram took his place on the edge of the set and when the director shouted "action," the actor charged into the scene, scowling.

"What the hell are you doing here?" Bram's character did a damn good job of emoting cold, hard fury.

Nico put his hand on the small of Lainie's back in an instinctive gesture at the guy's raised voice. Hadn't they signed on for a love scene?

Rosaria continued to flip cards. "I'm hunting for old ghosts, remember?"

Bram swiped the cards off the divan in silent fury, sending clubs and aces flying across the room. "I mean what the hell are you doing *here* in South Beach, tracking a goddamn killer without me?"

"You think you're my ace in the hole, Slick?" She flicked away the last card she'd held in her hand. "Think again."

Nico's eyes darted to Lainie, wondering what she thought of the heroine calling the guy Slick—the same not-so-freaking flattering name Lainie called him. For that matter, the movie's title *Diva's Last Dance*, reminded him that the heroine was probably the diva. Just like Lainie.

But she seemed not to notice, or was too taken up with the scene to care. Her green eyes remained riveted on the action in front of them as Bram hauled the heroine to her feet, his hands squeezing her upper arms with convincing force.

''Must be you've forgotten what kind of ace I'm packing.''

Even Ms. Calm, Cool and Collected Lainie looked surprised when the guy reached into his pants.

6

LAINIE DIDN'T CARE how big a movie star Bram Hawthorne might be, she was going to sue him and the
whole production company if he withdrew anything
male and naked from his shorts. He reached deeper,
wrapped his hand around some sort of rod—

Lainie held her breath.

—and pulled out a handgun.

Whew. She glanced up at Nico who'd somehow
moved much too close to her, but in the dark privacy
of the theaterlike setting, she didn't bother saying anything about it. She couldn't deny a rush of pleasure
when he'd put an arm around her as the scene started.
And now he winked at her as Bram's character dis-
cussed his weapon, his travails with Mexican drug run-
ners to retrieve it and his fervent hope Rosaria would
show a little bit of gratitude for his efforts.

She greeted his words with a huff and a flounce,
spinning away from her pursuer. "I won't kiss your
ass, no matter what I owe you, so you can just forget
it."

"Then how about I kiss yours instead?" He slid the
gun to a side table and stalked closer to the woman.

Lainie had to admit Rosaria Graham didn't fit her
idea of an adult-film star at all. First of all, she was an
extremely competent actress. And although she was
every bit as stacked as former Club Paradise cigarette

girl, Daisy Stephenson, the rest of her was athletic and agile looking. Exuding strength and grace, she prowled around the small set exchanging verbal barbs with the hero, a man her character didn't seem to fully trust.

Smart woman.

The cameras moved around the scene, occasionally impeding Lainie's view. But she could see everything perfectly when the heroine flipped him the middle finger. And when the hero lunged for her again.

Lainie hadn't expected to see a fight scene, but she had to admit there was a sensual edge about it as Bram tackled Rosaria. As Rosaria tackled him back. They rolled across the bed, exchanging positions of dominance, until they hit the floor with a thud.

Was that scripted?

The couple panted and cursed, kicking over a small table and dislodging a basket of blindfolds that Lainie knew were normally kept in a cabinet as props in the room. There was something decadent and undeniably sexual about the strewn blindfolds and the struggling couple. Their breathing grew heavier as she yelled at him for ditching her in a hotel room in California and he cursed at her for having a death wish.

And then he kissed her.

Not a sweet, melting kiss, but a kiss of bold, unapologetic domination. Out of the corner of her eye, she saw Daisy Stephenson stiffen, but she couldn't afford to give it much thought right now since the kiss seemed to be affecting her, too. She didn't realize how much until Nico's hand slid around her waist and up beneath her jacket.

It came to rest on the black-lace teddy she'd worn beneath her power suit today.

Pleasure rolled through her. Her belly. Her thighs.

She could almost feel his touch in those places, *wanted* to feel his touch in those places. The hungry, achy tingle of her skin made her breasts tighten, her nipples crest to stiff peaks.

The heat from his body seeped through his clothes, calling to her. The scent of him—the antibacterial soap and the faded, musky aftershave—filled her nostrils. If they were really watching this movie in a darkened theater she would seriously consider crawling into his lap right now and searching out the hard planes of his body with her hands. Molding herself to him until she lined them up chest to chest, hip to hip. Hell, maybe she'd just straddle him and ride him until she worked this hungry demon out of her.

Rosaria and Bram were peeling one another's clothes away. Her blouse flew across the room. His shirt popped buttons and slid off his arms. They still rolled around the carpet, crushing the strewn blindfolds beneath them as they wrestled for position. Rosaria's bare arms flexed, her triceps taut and lean as she pushed Bram's big shoulders to the floor.

Lainie noticed Daisy backing away from the scene, but Lainie couldn't take her eyes off it. She wondered if she could ever be that aggressive in bed. The wild struggle tantalized her, called to some long-denied urge inside her. She'd always striven to be in charge of her professional life, thriving on commendations and accolades the way other people thrived on food and water. What if she took all that self-ambition and released it in another direction?

Her heart slugged a heavy response to the thought even as Nico's hand rose, his fingers brushing along the underside of her lace-covered breasts. Could he feel the thudding of her pulse? Did he guess how her skin chafed to be free of that lace and spill into his hands? His mouth.

Lainie stood paralyzed by Nico's touch in the darkened periphery of the action. He shouldn't be doing this to her. Not when other guest viewers stood nearby in their cordoned-off area. Yet it felt delicious. Decadent. And well deserved.

She'd been without for so long. Even during her marriage, especially the last year when she'd been denying that her husband could be cheating on her yet had known in her heart he probably was, Lainie had avoided physical contact with him wherever possible. She hadn't wanted his hands on her when they might have just been on another woman.

Sex went to hell in a hurry under those circumstances.

To have a man's hand on her now, his thumb drawing small circles on her rib cage while his pinky stretched almost to the waistband of her skirt, the sensation made her weak with want. Even feisty Rosaria slowed down her fight when Bram brought his thigh up between her legs. He held it hard against her, his fingers already manipulating the zipper of her leather pants.

Lainie went wet with wanting, envisioning her and Nico that way. Her thighs spread wide by his legs. His hard body poised over her soft, aching curves. Or, better yet, his hard body underneath her while she remembered every sexual urge she'd ever repressed in the last two long years.

"Cut!" The director's voice made her jump.

Nico's hand fell away from her as the actor and actress broke apart as easily as if they'd been engaged in backgammon instead of foreplay. Someone clicked on a lamp near the guest viewers, making Lainie blink and squint as she fought her way out of intense daydreams.

"Let's go." Nico drew her toward the exit by her arm before she was ready to leave. She'd only barely exchanged niceties with the set director when they'd arrived. But then again, she didn't feel on her game after the scene they'd just watched. After the secret touches in the dark.

Squeezing out into the hotel corridor after nominal thank-yous to the film crew, they found some breathing room.

They weren't the first ones. Lainie could see Daisy walking away from the Fun & Games Chamber with her spine stiff and her gait hurried. Apparently she hadn't enjoyed the scene as much as Lainie had.

"Where can we go?" Nico's question brought her attention back to him as he glared down at her with a fierce expression.

"I don't know what you mean." She couldn't have a discussion with him now. Not after whatever had just happened in there between them.

Her hormones were not only reawakened, they were neglected, starved and cranky as hell after the ridiculously long hiatus. She couldn't afford to have any conversation in which they played a contributing role.

"You know damn well what I mean and we need to talk about this." He steered her across the Persian carpet toward the elevator bank. "Which will it be—your office or your suite?"

The doors opened before them and Lainie panicked just a little. "I can't get in an elevator with you like this."

He held up his hands. "I promise I won't treat the

elevator like a food-supply closet. Just tell me where we can go for some privacy.''

Desire pooled low in her belly at the thought of taking him back to her rooms. Of being wild and aggressive with Nico Cesare.

She couldn't take him to her suite. That sent all the wrong messages—both to him and her hungry libido. Then again, she couldn't take him to her office where a thousand and one employees seemed to congregate whenever they ran into a problem. What if her libido got the best of her and she jumped Nico right before a co-worker strode through the door?

Stepping into the elevator, she made up her mind. ''Fourth floor. We can talk in my suite, but only long enough to clear up any mixed signals we've got going back and forth between us.''

Nico followed her into the small lift lined with shirred, salmon-colored silk. He stabbed the necessary button until number four lit up. His jaw clenched as he turned to glare at her. ''Trust me, there won't be any confusion about the message I'm sending after today.''

Oh.

O-kay.

Lainie stared at him as waves of heat and obvious sexual frustration rolled off him in waves. She knew she shouldn't send mixed messages to a man on the edge. And she planned on making herself very clear once they got back to her room.

But until then, she had hormones bubbling in her veins, too, and her wants were no less urgent than his. Telling herself she had one more floor and ten more yards to go before she needed to act on logic, Lainie took a step closer to all that male heat.

''What if I tell you that, like it or not, I don't have

a clue what message to send back to you?'' She moved in as near as she dared without getting burned. ''What if I know in my head that anything between us is impossible, yet that doesn't stop me from wanting to drag you into my bed and lock you up for twenty-four hours of our own fun and games?''

Nico felt his right eye begin to tremble. Twitch. Throb with the pounding beat of a pulse gone rogue.

The elevator chimed its arrival on Lainie's floor just as his eyes started to cross with lust. Latching onto her arm, he hauled her out of the elevator before he realized he had no idea where to go next.

''Right. All the way at the end.'' She already clutched her room key in her free hand.

''Do you have any idea what a mammoth gauntlet you just tossed me back there?'' He fumed and hoped he didn't foam at the mouth. ''I can't take any more of your brand of fun and games. No more of this red light, green light bullshit.''

After yanking the card out of her hand, he opened the door. He knew the Club Paradise employees all called this suite The Diva Penthouse in honor of its resident, but he'd never even been up to this floor before. He'd been so annoyed about his sister working in such an oversexed environment that he'd pretty much stuck to the kitchen when he'd visited her here. Now that Giselle had left the States to travel abroad with her boyfriend, Nico finally realized how shortsighted and selfish his views had been.

All the more reason not to be shortsighted and self-serving now. Sure, it would be easy to haul Lainie up against him after her provocation, but how long would he have before she came to her senses? Before she booted him out and locked him out of her life for good?

"Red light, green light?" She followed him into her suite, tossing her leather binder on a small sideboard near the front door. The rooms looked as if they hadn't yet been renovated, the living area a collection of bold seventies furnishings against a backdrop of gold walls and taupe carpet while the kitchen maintained a forties art deco sensibility. Shiny white cabinets and bright silver drawer pulls looked so retro they could almost have been modern except for the well-worn linoleum flooring.

His gaze moved to the doorway leading to her bedroom and a neat white bedspread, but he didn't dare go there with the tension running high between them. After steering her toward the safer terrain of the sofa, he waited for her to take a seat and then lowered himself to the solid block of unadorned wood right in front of her that served as a coffee table.

"You know, stop and go. The kiss outside the hotel after the 'we need to part ways' speech. The kiss in the kitchen pantry and then you ditch me. The heavy breathing and the heart palpitations I could feel right here." He slammed his own chest with his palm, even though he was actually referring to her chest. Which he couldn't actually look at right now if he expected to maintain his grip on reason. "Then in the elevator, you toss out this huge land mine of 'I'm not sure, but sex sounds great.' Jesus, woman. I think I burst a blood vessel or six."

"So sue me for being honest." She leaned back on the sofa, but Nico guessed her stance had more to do with putting space between them than making herself comfortable.

"Actually, I can appreciate honesty since all I ever heard from my last girlfriend's mouth was lies, apparently. But you can't just toss out a comment like that—'' Something niggled at his brain. ''Wait a minute. You're saying all that stuff about dragging me into bed is you being honest?''

Lightbulbs went off in his head. Not just lightbulbs, mammoth neon signs started flashing through his consciousness. And they all spelled out messages that the opportunity for great sex loomed nearby.

''Honest but shortsighted, I realize.'' She stared down at her nails as if contemplating a new manicure, but he knew damn well she was just avoiding eye contact. He knew how much it sucked to feel vulnerable.

Carefully adjusting the three rings on her right hand so that the stones sat in perfect alignment with her knuckles, she continued. ''I've learned not to act on my every impulse, but when temptation comes along, sometimes it's difficult to remember my ultimate goals.''

''You care to share these goals with me since they seem to be tripping me up at every turn?'' Frustration itched at him, but it couldn't block the hunger for her. He'd slowly grown obsessed with this woman who was so fiercely independent that she didn't need him. Didn't even recognize his NHL connection until he'd spelled it out for her. Maybe after years of having women purposely seek him out because of his fame, he just wanted to experience the thrill of the chase again.

And not just that. He wanted to deliberately do the picking and choosing. He'd had the opportunity to see Lainie in action without her knowing, to watch her manage Club Paradise with finesse and intelligence. She was so much different from Ashley or any other woman he'd been with.

''I want to maintain the best property on the strip.''

She leaned forward now, obviously not afraid to get close to him when it came to spelling out her all-important goals. ''I want to make back every penny I lost in my divorce from a cheating liar—not because I need that money, but just to show the world that I can. I want to be strong and self-sufficient, and I don't ever want to deceive myself into a bad situation again just because it looks nice from the outside.''

They were so close he could almost feel the force of her conviction. Her rich, complex scent teased his nose. He spied a tiny scar on her forehead he'd never seen before. The delicate white line reminded him that no matter how much she talked a big game, Lainie Reynolds had been hurt before.

''You don't want much, do you?'' His hand reached for her forehead and that narrow jagged line before he could stop himself. Smoothing the soft skin with his thumb, he eased over the old wound and wished it could be that simple to absorb the hurt that went with it.

''On the contrary, Slick, I want a whole hell of a lot.'' Her voice dropped to a throaty note. ''But I've learned the hard way that some of the things I want aren't necessarily good for me.''

''True enough.'' His fingers sifted through her hair, tracking along the back of her scalp and then down to her neck. The smooth column of her throat. ''But did it ever occur to you that maybe you're looking too much at the long-term goals and not enough at the short term?''

A shot in the dark, perhaps, but desperate times called for desperate measures. And Nico got the impression that Lainie could be swayed if only he found the right way for her to justify going after what she wanted.

"I don't understand." She frowned. "I have all my goals broken down into manageable, achievable parcels. There's a six-month scale, a yearly plan, a five-year plan...I've been very thorough."

"What about a short-term goal for saving your sanity while you work on the never-ending 'to do' lists? Have you ever considered maybe you need to reward yourself throughout the journey in order to make it more fun?"

"Fun?" She raised a skeptical brow.

"That's a radical concept for you?" Maybe there was a small place in her life for him after all. She needed him without even realizing it.

"I just fail to see how it's going to further my big-picture ambitions."

"Maybe it can save you from burning out before you reach those ambitions of yours. What good are the plans and the goals divvied up into tidy package deals if they make you want to tear your hair out before you can achieve them because all you're doing is working nonstop?" His older brother Vito had once given him the very same lecture when Nico had been working his ass off toward achieving a spot with the Panthers. He'd changed his position four times in a season because he kept hearing different things about what the Miami hockey team might be scouting for.

Funny how the lecture made a hell of a lot more sense when giving than receiving. Nico had ended up in a huge fight with the oldest Cesare and they hadn't spoken for nearly a week—a time frame roughly equivalent to forever in a household filled with talk.

"So you're saying that I shouldn't look at sex as a

potential obstacle to trip me up, but an outlet for fun that will inspire me to continue on my quest.''

''I guess so, but I hope you won't be offended if I say that my words sounded a hell of a lot more eloquent than yours.'' He'd been rather proud of his spiel until she'd boiled it down to the most basic terms possible.

''It's called cutting through the BS, and it's invaluable when practicing law or dealing with agenda-driven men. But you know what?'' She smiled. A no-holds-barred, undiluted grin that he'd never seen before.

''What?'' He stared at this new side of The Diva. He couldn't be sure, but there was a distinct possibility his heart skipped a beat.

''I think I like this plan of yours.''

LAINIE HAD ACQUIRED plenty of negotiating skills in law school, skills she'd honed to razor-sharp perfection while a practicing corporate attorney. But one of the most important and overlooked areas of expertise in negotiation was knowing when to say enough is enough and simply close the deal.

Based on a wealth of experience, therefore, she knew this was the time to just shut up and seal the bargain. She slid forward on the dark leather couch.

''**You** do?'' Nico sounded as if he didn't believe her. And who could blame him when she'd purposely removed her emotions from their discussion today?

Or at least, she'd removed them enough so the untrained eye could never see them. But that didn't mean they weren't there, coloring her decisions no matter how hard she tried to ignore them.

''I do.'' Her heart slugged hard against her chest. Half scared and half thrilled to have made up her mind to pursue some fun, even if the justification rated as flimsy at best, Lainie thought maybe the best way to explain what she wanted would be a demonstration Nico couldn't misunderstand. "You said it yourself. If we do this, it's going to be for the sake of fun, right?"

She reached for the button of her jacket on instinct. Nico's eyes had strayed to the lace peeking above her jacket more than once today, making her hope he'd like to see more. The black teddy she wore underneath was imported silk and lace, a decidedly feminine piece that helped give new life to her conservative suit. It was the kind of undergarment that deserved to be seen.

She leaned forward to edge her way out of the sleeves when Nico made a croaking sound.

His eyes riveted to her breasts, he whispered under his breath. "Slow down, lady. I've been fantasizing about this ever since you wore those black leather pants the day you turned in your ex to the police."

Not exactly a happy memory for her, but she could overlook his odd sense of timing for the sake of the new information it uncovered. Letting her jacket slide down her shoulders with painstaking deliberation, Lainie watched him carefully.

"You've been thinking about me since then?" She had barely registered his presence that day other than to tell him off when she thought he might be in cahoots with Robert.

And all this time, he'd been remembering her.

"Ass-kicking never looked so good." He ran a finger along one lace strap of her exposed teddy. "You dethroned every last one of Charlie's Angels—past and present."

Shivers of anticipation danced over her skin. She'd

never been any man's fantasy before. Maybe—just in the spirit of fun, of course—she could be this man's.

Inspired by the movie scene they'd watched earlier, she decided now was as good a time as any to go for the gusto. She ran her hand down his chest and hooked a finger in his belt before giving the leather a tug.

"Then load your weapon, Slick. You can come along for the ride on my next adventure if you've got what it takes."

7

HER WORDS SET OFF A FIRESTORM.

Nico's hands were streaking down her back, curving around her waist and sliding over her belly, her ribs and oooh…her breasts. His musky scent filled her nostrils along with the heated aroma of her perfume. The two fragrances melded and merged the way their bodies would soon, blending until they became one.

His lips descended on hers, sparking a chain reaction of liquid warmth throughout her whole body. His kiss was chemistry in motion, firing away her defenses and leaving her a simmering mass of need.

She slid forward on the couch, and Nico pulled her up into his lap where he sat on the wooden chest that served as her coffee table. She ended up crossways against him, her shoulder to his chest, one hip tucked against the hard length of his erection. His hands continued to map her body, surveying the curves and dips with hard palms and questing fingers.

Desire rolled over her, too fast and too furious to tamp down. Feminine sexual energy charged to life with frightening intensity. Her hormones roared and surged as she clung to Nico's shoulders, desperate for more. Soon. Now.

His fingers found her nipple through the black-lace teddy she wore. He tweaked the taut crest and sent a jolt of longing deep inside her. She unbuttoned his shirt and then hitched her fingers around the straps of her outfit, ready for skin-to-skin contact.

"Wait." He stopped her before she could bare so much as a shoulder. "I want to be able to really see you."

And she wanted to be able to really feel him. But she couldn't have formed words right then if she tried. She merely moved to the buckle on his belt until he rose, hauling her and her out-of-control desire across the room.

Where? She blinked, confused as he bypassed the door to her bedroom and strode to the terrace of her fourth-floor apartment.

"Are you okay with us going outside?" Nico had already toed the sliding-glass door open with his foot. "I want to see you and I don't think a table lamp can compare to the Florida sun."

As if she could deny him anything now when her thighs itched to wrap around his waist and her sex ached to have him deep inside her. She unglued her tongue from the roof of her mouth. "Outside is good. I don't have any condoms, though."

She hadn't even thought about sex in a year. Okay, maybe she'd thought about it a time or two. But she sure hadn't planned on having it. She hadn't realized how much animal lust she'd been storing away all this time.

"I've got one." He angled them through the terrace door and into the relentless Florida sunshine. "I can go out later for more."

"Good idea." She plunged her fingers underneath his shirt and skimmed her hands across his bare chest.

"We'll need a case at least." He set her down in one of two wooden deck loungers strewn with blue-

and-white striped cushions, then stripped off his shirt. He stared down at her with dark, smoldering eyes. "Damn but you're hot."

She reached out for him, waggling her fingers impatiently. "How would you know when you're not even close enough to touch?"

He fell on her with a speed that must have done his sport proud. God knows it pleased her to no end. He stretched out next to her on the lounger, the heavy Adirondack furnishing one of many incongruities in her mismatched suite.

Right now, however, she was damn grateful to have it. She couldn't imagine why Nico needed this much light to see her. She was practically blinded by the afternoon sun despite the healthy overhang of roof providing some shade on the terrace.

He molded his body to hers as they lay on their sides, facing one another. His hand tugged down the zipper on her skirt. "How about this? Is this close enough?"

"Not nearly, and you know it." She wriggled her hips to ease the zipper down all the faster. "Don't start something you can't finish."

Steering the skirt over her hips and down her thighs, he stared into her eyes as if he could see every secret hidden inside her. "Don't you worry about me finishing. I'm just going to make damn sure it's you who finishes first." He stared down at her body clad only in her teddy. "You're beautiful."

Her heart caught awkwardly in her chest at the compliment. She'd been okay when he told her she was hot. She was not okay with "you're beautiful." It was a loaded sentiment, an intimate compliment.

She didn't want to feel beautiful when she was with

Nico. She simply needed to be desired. Wanted. Lusted over.

But Nico's gaze lingered on her. Ate her up. Lavished silent compliments on her that were a sure path to heartache if she was foolish enough to listen.

Redirect. Redirect.

She lifted her fingers to the V of her cleavage and trickled them down the center of her body, over her ribs. She flattened her palm out over her belly, touching herself with a hand that trembled just a little. Pausing as her fingers grazed the top of her lace-covered mound she stared up at him to gauge his reaction.

On target.

Nico's eyes went almost black as he stared at the progress of her hand. Then, levering himself up on one elbow beside her, he yanked her lace outfit off her shoulder.

His mouth found her breast while she eased off the remaining shoulder of the teddy. And then his mouth sought her other breast, circling the tightened nipple until she cried out.

The sultry breeze off the ocean carried away the sound, but even if the terrace beneath them had been full of hotel guests, Lainie wouldn't have cared. No one could see them with the thick stucco wall sheltering their lounge chair. And there were no buildings close enough to provide a view of their activities. Only a handful of potted hibiscus plants stood sentinel to Nico's feast and her near nakedness.

She couldn't get enough of him. Her hands tugged and unzipped their way into his pants, freeing the bulge that had been jabbing her hip. Reaching into his boxers, she stroked the velvety hard length of him as he kissed and sucked her breasts.

So good.

Her finger circled the tip of his cock and the wetness she found there. She slicked over the top of him and felt her womb contract in hungry answer.

"You're moving at hyperspeed, lady." Nico groaned as she touched him, his body growing impossibly longer, harder in her hands.

"Once I make up my mind about something—ooh…" She sighed out her satisfaction as he palmed her breast and shoved the black lace to her waist. "I tend to move forward with decisive action."

Skimming her hand down the lace, she urged the fabric lower. She wanted nothing more than to lie skin to skin with him, to absorb the heat and restless male energy of him through her skin.

"Decisive is good." He dragged the garment down her legs and flung it over the lounger. "But next time we take things slower." He sketched featherlight touches up the inside of her thigh, sending pulses of pleasure through her veins. "That way I can take in all the nuances."

"Next time." She made the promise mindlessly. Later she would worry about next time. Decide if there should be a next time. God, she hoped so. "I can't wait now. It's been too long."

She peered up at him long enough to see his gaze soften, his eyes light with empathy. Damn it, she didn't want his compassion. Just the passion part, please. She couldn't deal with emotions now.

To emphasize the point, she stroked the length of him, curving her hand around the erection she wanted inside her.

His focus dimmed, glazed for satisfying seconds. "Understood."

He shoved boxers, trousers and belt down his legs. Off the end of the lounger. And then he was on top of her, pressing her more deeply into the cotton broadcloth of the lounger cushions, his body aligned with hers.

The sunlight glared against her closed eyelids for a moment before Nico's shadow descended over her, his body blocking the sun. His presence next to her blocking out all other thoughts except connecting to him in the most elemental way.

"Please, please, please." She chanted the words as his cock rubbed up against her thigh, the velvety length of him sending spasms of pleasure coursing through her. Heat built deep inside her.

"Soon." His low growl thrummed in the air around them, his breath fanning over her skin and raising goose bumps. "I don't want you to be so decisive you miss out on the best parts of this."

He reached between her thighs, plucked the feminine flesh and she nearly came out of her skin. A moan ripped from her throat, a rusty cry that hadn't been called from her lips since—hell, since ever. She'd never had this much hot lust screaming through her, demanding release. Tension coiled high inside her and for a fleeting instant she wondered—worried—what Nico would think of her wild response. But she couldn't spare it any more thought now, not with the heat beating down on her skin, Nico spreading her wide with powerful legs and his fingers touching the most sensitive part of her.

She pried her eyes open to see him, to try and slow herself down. Nico stared at her with a mixture of intense heat and dark emotion in his gaze.

God, but he was gorgeous. The knowledge that he wanted her every bit as much as she wanted him...

The tight coil inside her snapped, held her paralyzed for one long, sensation-drenched second, before unfurling in an endless chain of delicious spasms. The contractions rocked her, jolted her. She cried out until her voice went hoarse, and even when she finally lay still, Nico would move his finger ever so slightly against her and more delicious spasms would squeeze deep inside her.

She was a mess. A total wreck. A candidate for love slavery if she didn't snap out of it soon. But even as she yelled at herself in her mind, her body remained prone beneath him, sprawled and wanton and more than willing to give him more.

"See?" His voice hummed against her ear, stirring her. "You wouldn't have wanted to miss the best part."

A slow smile slid over her face even if she couldn't manage to lift her eyelids again. "You've got it all wrong, Slick." Her hand found the thick length of his cock pressed against her thigh. Stroked. "This is the best part."

Nico closed his eyes and hoped he could survive more of Lainie's touches. She'd nearly launched him into orbit with her sure grip and knowing fingers earlier. And now that he'd watched her unravel in his arms, he was already hanging by a thread. Never in his whole life had he seen anything sexier than Ms. Calm and Controlled shedding every last one of her inhibitions along with her clothes. He'd expected her to be aggressive in bed, but he hadn't counted on the wildness, the ability to let go so completely.

Now she guided him to her sex, urged him inside when he wasn't ready.

"Wait." He scrambled for his pants, wishing he'd had the presence of mind to fish out the lone condom he carried when he first brought her out to the terrace.

"I can't wait." The longing in her voice mirrored every instinct he possessed, but the need to protect her was too strong. Too damn important.

"I just need to—" He found the condom just in time.

She was pressing him against the heated center of her, rubbing his cock all around her slick folds until he nearly lost his mind.

He nearly dropped the condom five different times thanks to his focus being divided between what he was trying to do and what she was trying so damn sweetly to do. But finally, he was ready to go, needing her so damn bad he thought he'd lose his mind.

Balancing himself over her, he nudged his way inside. The afternoon sun blistered his back, nothing in comparison to the heat emanating from Lainie Reynolds's delectable body. She lifted herself up on her elbows, rising to meet his every thrust.

He'd brought her out into the light so he could see every bit of her, to see past her cool exterior to the woman she was beneath. Now that he had a glimpse, he knew he'd never look at her the same way. Would never be content to only see a part of her again.

He gripped the wooden slats along the back of the lounge chair and hauled himself higher against her. Pushed himself deeper inside. Lainie's thighs followed his, her long legs wrapping around his and pulling him more tightly to her.

He bent to taste her, to kiss her lips, her neck. She

arched her back, pushing her breasts up closer to his chest. He licked his finger, then twirled it around one taut nipple until another wild moan ripped from her throat and her body spasmed all around him.

Control wasn't even an option.

With Lainie's legs squeezing his waist and her sex pulsing around his, Nico hurtled over the edge in a free fall.

JUST AS THE LOUNGER TIPPED. Backward. Headfirst. They toppled down to the concrete in a tangle of arms and legs and damned if the solid thud of their landing didn't even come close to halting the momentum of his release. Or hers.

He cradled her head even though the cushion slid right out of the upended chair along with them. And still they moaned. Cried out. Kissed as if they couldn't possibly devour one another fast enough.

Nico knew he was being selfish to hold her there, savoring the scent of her hair in his nose as he absorbed the feel of her skin against his body. But he'd waited too damn long for this intimate connection to give her up easily. Even if she was probably uncomfortable as hell.

Ah damn.

Pulling away even though his hormones protested loudly, Nico rose to right the lounger and steady a teetering hibiscus in a terra-cotta pot. He reached to scoop up the cushion and the flushed, sexy-as-hell woman still reclining on it.

"That's okay." Lainie held him off with one manicured hand, the gesture reminding him of the Club Paradise CEO, the reigning South Beach diva.

Except that she was still naked.

Nico didn't even blink as she rose, her lean hips and full breasts looking totally at home without clothes. But before he could salivate himself parched he realized maybe they should be a little more discreet. The shorn hairs at the back of his neck prickled, making him whirl around to make sure no one else was being treated to the show. He'd worked his ass off to put himself in Lainie's line of sight. No way would he share the rewards of that effort with anyone else.

"Maybe we ought to go inside." He blocked her body with the breadth of his, unable to shake the feeling of being watched. "I wouldn't want to give the birds whiplash."

She glanced down at his member and smiled. "Neither would I. You'd better bring that in here."

Crooking her finger at him, she backed into the hotel suite, still full of that wild streak that had taken him by surprise. Hot damn.

His member was in the door before him.

She was already down the short corridor to the bedroom and he had to squint to see her. The sway of her hips snagged his eye as she turned the corner into the bedroom, pausing only to make sure he followed.

Her moves were like testosterone injections, fueling him on, even though he had the sneaking suspicion that sex with Lainie was only going to tie him up in knots and make everything more complicated.

He'd thought maybe great sex would be a good way to heal after the number her ex-husband had done on her. And hell, after the way Ashley had pulled the rug out from under him. He needed to get his head on straight and figure out what he wanted in a relationship eventually. But for right now, just sex had sounded safe. Therapeutic. And, because it was with Lainie, enticing as hell.

But already the sex was rocking his whole world. Tipping him on his ass faster than any upended deck lounger. Still, here he was, chasing her down the hallway and into her bedroom as fast as his feet could take him.

He caught her just beyond the door, banding his arms around her from behind. Her yelp of surprise didn't faze him, but her wriggling her way out of his arms did.

Releasing her near the monochromatic white bed in the sleek white room, he wondered what he'd missed. "I don't get it. Do you want me to stay?"

While he willed her to say yes, she sidestepped away from him. "Don't you remember the scene we watched today? I don't know about you, but the thought of playing cat and mouse sort of fired me up." She twirled a lock of hair around her finger as if she had all the time in the world to think about her personal turn-ons.

Obviously she didn't realize she'd already turned him on and he was very much ready to go.

"Cat and mouse, is it?" He went very still, calculating the number of steps between them. Planning his strategy of attack. "I hope you know which role I'm playing."

She arched an eyebrow. Stretched up on her toes to stand taller. "It's abundantly clear to *me* since I couldn't be a mouse if my life depended on it."

Stalking closer, he kept her in his sights as she backed around the bed. "Maybe you could say the same about me. Besides, I'm not the one running away right now."

He had her cornered next to the bed and she had no choice but to stop. Face him.

"Maybe I didn't leave enough claw marks on you last time." She traced her nails lightly over his shoulders, scraping them down his arms with a feathery caress. "Guess I'll have to fix that in round two."

He didn't think it was possible to want a woman this much ten minutes after he'd had her the first time. Damn it, it hadn't been possible since he was nineteen and perpetually horny. Yet here he was, ready, willing and eager as hell to have her all over him again.

"Don't forget round two belongs to me." He reached for her, ready to set aside any cat-and-mouse games so he could lose himself in her.

"Says who?" Scrambling away in a blur of naked limbs, she scooted across the bed and landed on her feet on the other side before he could touch her.

"Says me, damn it. I called it right up front in round one." How the hell had she gotten by him? He shook off a fraction of the lust fog and reminded himself he'd have to be better prepared if he wanted to catch her next time. "That was a hell of a move, by the way."

"Cats are quick." She ran her hand through her hair, smoothing the strands that had become tousled out on the terrace. "And I don't recall you claiming round two for your own."

"It's not just for me." His muscles flexed and tightened, sliding into pounce position as he eased his way around the bed again. "It's going to be very much for you."

Her already taut, rosy nipples stiffened even more as he spoke. Damn but he loved that. He hastened his step, keeping his eye on the goal.

"For me?" She swallowed as she backed up another step. Collided with the wall behind her.

"Total, nonstop pleasure for the Club Paradise diva." His hands itched to touch her again. To hold her still while his mouth roved all over, discovered every sweet hollow and luscious curve.

"I'm no diva." She shook her head, apparently familiar with her nickname. "I've always been more behind the scenes than in the spotlight."

"But from what I gather, you're the real power behind the operation." He had her locked in his sights now. There would be no easy escape for her, which was a damn good thing considering he needed her again so badly he couldn't think about anything else. "You know a lot of people think that kind of power is very sexy?"

"Yeah? A lot of guys think a woman with power equals a megabitch from hell." She held her head high as she lobbed the verbal bomb, but Nico heard the hint of vulnerability behind the words.

"Only guys with overinflated egos who can't handle the idea of a woman above them." He was close enough to see the quick rise and fall of her chest, to smell her lightly exotic fragrance. His hands reached. Slowly. Carefully.

"What about a guy who can't even stand to play mouse to her cat?"

Damn. His hands fell back to his sides. Time was of the essence in answering a loaded question like that, so he tried not to overthink it.

"Are you kidding? I'd love to have a woman above me." He knew he'd probably failed the test when she rolled her eyes, but damn it, he'd given it his best shot. "Especially if the woman happens to be you."

She stared up at him with bright green eyes that didn't miss a trick. ''Good. Then you won't mind giving me a piece of round two.''

Hooking her foot around his ankle, she leaped on top of him in a pounce that would have done any cat proud.

And left him with an armful of naked woman.

Her breasts perched invitingly above his mouth, he arched up for a taste, licking a path down the valley of her cleavage.

''Honey, I might have been the victim of an over-inflated ego a time or two, but I would never be stupid enough to turn down a gorgeous woman who wanted to jump me.'' His hands ran over her hips, around her waist, up the creamy expanse of her back. ''And did a damn good job of it, I might add.''

She stretched up over him and lifted herself off him until her breasts just barely skimmed his chest. Then, edging backward on her hands and knees she slid her body down the length of his, teasing his skin with those taut nipples of hers until her breasts straddled his cock.

Holy— She was killing him. He didn't know if she was going to shock him into a heart attack with her unexpected wild side, or if she would simply screw his brains out.

He hoped for the latter.

''I'm so glad you're giving me high marks on my moves.'' She cupped her breasts around his cock, squeezing them against him. ''You'll have to let me know what you think of this.''

He couldn't have answered her if his life depended on it. Thinking wasn't even an option. In fact, any type of brain function seemed impossible when all his blood surged south in a tidal wave of pure lust.

She hovered above him, deliberately darting her pink tongue all around her lips.

Oh yes.

But before he could feel the damp thrill of her tongue on him, an explosion rocked through him so hard he feared he'd unmanned himself.

Even Lainie looked confused. Worried.

She was sliding off him just as a second explosion sounded in time with shouts and screams from all over the hotel.

8

LAINIE HAD NO MEMORY of how she put her clothes on. She had a vague impression of Nico handing her shoes to her and opening her front door for her, but other than that, she couldn't say how she'd ended up in the red-linen sheath dress that she wore now as she and Nico pounded down four flights of stairs, following the scent of smoke.

Fear threatened to choke her faster than the gray haze wafting up the stairwell. Nico dialed 911 while they ran. She called Brianne while her fingers shook, her brain failing to remember the right combination of numbers three times over.

Hotel guests ran past them as they burst through the steel door onto the first floor. Smoke and dust floated in the air, clogging the lobby with an acrid gray cloud.

Sirens blared outside, probably only a few blocks away. A throng of people congregated around the coffee shop that opened out onto the lobby near one of the hotel's three restaurants. Through the crowd, Lainie spied Brianne Wolcott's distinctive auburn hair towering above the majority of people around her. At five foot eleven in bare feet, Brianne dwarfed the rest of her fellow owners.

Relieved, Lainie disconnected her cell-phone call that wasn't going through anyhow. She tried to push her way through the mass of curious onlookers stand-

ing near the source of the drifting smoke, but she didn't
have any luck until Nico took up the charge. Those
wide shoulders cleared a path for her instantly, plowing
through rubberneckers and other assorted gawkers.

''Bri!'' She shouted to her friend, not realizing until
she was almost on top of her that ambience coordinator
Summer Farnsworth was right there beside her, her
kinky blond curls tied back in a blue ribbon, a smudge
of ashes across one cheek. ''Is everyone okay? What
happened?''

''An explosion in the kitchen.'' Summer answered
while Brianne talked on her two-way radio, clearing an
entrance for the firefighters who had just arrived on the
scene.

''Explosion?'' Could it have been a grease fire?

''I think the new chef candidate might have been
hurt. One second I was standing next to her, handing
her a bunch of bananas for bananas Foster, and the next
second the whole kitchen blasted into pieces.'' Summer's eyes turned watery and red. ''I haven't seen her
since then.''

The fear that had been tingling in Lainie's belly rose
up to tremble through her whole body. She would have
beelined to the kitchen—or whatever remained of the
kitchen—to find the woman herself, but Brianne was
already directing a stream of firefighters to head that
way. Even Brianne's fiancé, an unconventional FBI
agent who rode a Harley and had reportedly just had
Bri's name tattooed across his hip, emerged on the
scene.

''I'm going back there.'' Nico started to follow the
trail of people headed to the kitchen when Lainie's cell
phone rang.

''Not without me you're not. Wait up a minute.''

She yanked his arm to hold him back while she answered her phone with the other hand. "Hello?"

"I hear you're having some trouble over at the hotel today." The blast-from-the-past voice of her ex-husband, Robert Flynn, chilled her despite the residual heat rolling into the lobby from the kitchen.

She kept herself steady by staring straight into Nico Cesare's deep brown eyes. "And just what would you know about it, jailbird?"

"You should remember I have friends on the outside, Lainie." His clipped tone and precise elocution reminded her what a superficial jerk he could be. "And since I have you to thank for putting me behind bars, I couldn't help but gloat a little now that you're running into a few problems of your own."

The phone clicked in her ear and dead air took the place of his voice.

"Who was that?" Nico's hands gripped her shoulders, tension radiating through his whole body and into hers.

As if she wasn't tense enough already.

Fear knotted in her belly as Robert's words echoed in her ears. Scavenging some composure on a day rapidly descending from terrible to hellacious, Lainie took a deep breath before she found the words. "It was my ex calling from jail to rub it in about my bad luck, apparently. Don't they monitor phone calls from inmates or something so they don't terrorize the general population?"

"How the hell does he know your kitchen exploded twenty minutes after it happened?" Nico's eyebrows swooped down in a dark glare that would have been scary except that it was clearly anger on her behalf.

Fists clenched and neck muscles flexing, he looked ready to take her ex-husband apart.

And for some reason, all that male anger soothed her just a little.

"I don't know, but I'll call my attorney after we find out what happened here." Time to look into extra security for the hotel. She wouldn't let Robert's vindictiveness hurt anyone else—if he truly was behind this.

Her eyes searched the throng of firefighters and found the soot-covered South Beach fire chief striding her way.

"I'm sorry to be the bearer of bad news, but it looks like your kitchen is going to be out of commission for a while." The young fire chief tugged off her helmet, revealing a long dark braid and concerned expression. "The exterior walls look sound, but there's a hole in the floor and most of the countertop with the main appliances is completely demolished. We've got two casualties back there with broken limbs, but no fatalities."

No fatalities.

The words put the whole situation into perspective. Lainie should be relieved there were no fatalities. And she was, damn it. She just hadn't fully grasped how serious this situation might have been.

"Has anyone called the police?"

"Done." Nico spoke up this time, jaw clenched as he took in the chaos all around them. "I called them on my way down here and I thought I saw a squad car pull up a minute ago."

The fire chief nodded, shoving her helmet under one arm. "They'll need to speak to me first, but no doubt they'll seek you out afterward."

She took off through the crowded lobby, easing around dazed hotel guests in her heavy boots.

"They'll want to know about Flynn's call." Nico pitched his cell phone from hand to hand, restless with caged anger. "You want me to get you a Coke? Shoehorn people back to their rooms? Help Brianne? Jesus, Lainie, I need a job to do."

She stared up at the man she'd been naked with less than an hour ago. A man she barely knew, yet she'd shown him a side of her she hadn't even been sure existed anymore.

After the sparks they'd generated in her suite, she hadn't planned on letting their paths grow more entwined. She'd told herself she could have him only if they kept things simple, acknowledging that their relationship was a by-product of being on the rebound. Yet here they were, knee-deep in a catastrophe that made being without a chef look like child's play.

Now she didn't even have a damn kitchen. Or did she?

Telling herself this bond with Nico would only be temporary, she let a new plan of action take shape in her mind. A plan that would help the resort and give herself a little distance from him at the same time. A good thing considering all she really wanted to do now was run into those strong arms of his and hide for a few days.

"If you want a job, I've got about twenty of them. First and foremost is making sure my Hollywood guests don't leave, which means I may need your cooking expertise another day."

"Cooking?" He shook his head, scratching an impatient hand across his chest. "What do you want me to do, roast hot dogs over the open flames from the explosion?''

''Definitely not.'' She punched in a text message to Summer and Brianne while her brain finalized the details of a plan. They needed a meeting pronto. ''Club Paradise houses a second, smaller kitchen off the café. With three restaurants and a coffee shop, Giselle insisted on two kitchens even though she did all her work out of the main one.''

Nico nodded, shoulders relaxing slightly with the promise of an active role. ''I remember her saying she liked to try out recipes there. She considered it her private turf.''

''I'll order a gazillion lobsters and we'll have a big deck party tonight. By the time the newspapers are on the scene we'll be making lemonade with these lemons.'' She backed away from Nico and all the temptation that came along with him. She couldn't afford to lose herself in those broad shoulders, wouldn't allow herself to lean on any man again. Just as soon as she got this latest crisis under control she'd reassert herself as sole mistress of her destiny.

Until then, who would it hurt if she stockpiled a few earth-shattering orgasms for posterity's sake?

Taking another step back, she paused when Nico followed.

''What?''

''You can't leave yet. You haven't talked to the police.'' He signaled a uniformed officer who was just finishing up with the fire chief. ''If that bastard Flynn is somehow connected to this, we need to nail him.''

''*We?*''

Nico sensed the inevitable speech about setting boundaries coming on, but he'd be damned if he was going to listen to it. Ever since they'd been jarred out of her hotel suite thanks to the kitchen explosion, he knew she'd give him the talk about maintaining their independence from one another, but this was definitely not the time.

If he could just keep her distracted, maybe he could buy enough time to get her alone again before she decided she'd made a colossal mistake by sleeping with him.

Hell, *he* already had the sinking feeling they'd messed up by getting intimate too fast. Despite his time as a celebrated athlete, he'd defied the odds and hadn't slept with all that many women. He didn't have much experience separating sex from a deeper connection, and apparently he sucked at it because he was already feeling pretty damn connected to Lainie.

Given that she was carrying enough relationship baggage for both of them, that couldn't be a good thing.

"Yeah, *we*. I hate what that two-timing loser did to you and my sister." Mentioning Giselle seemed to soothe her ruffled feathers momentarily since she nodded in vague agreement.

And by then, thank God, the cops had arrived. He didn't care to overthink the whole Lainie issue right now when her hotel was falling down around her ears. Notebook in hand, one of the officers took down informal statements from both of them, including details about Lainie's call from her ex.

Jealousy raged through him as he thought about Robert Flynn, a bastard who didn't deserve to sleep with her shoes, let alone the rest of her. Damned strange how one scorching tangle on a deck lounger could inspire such protective feelings in a guy, but nevertheless, there it was. Lainie Reynolds might be the

Club Paradise CEO and diva extraordinaire to the rest of South Beach, but he had seen something else in her. Something more vulnerable.

He guessed she had let him see a side of her she rarely showed to anyone else.

The police officer, a Latino guy who made up in width what he lacked in height, closed his notebook. "We'll stop by the jail to find out more about the alleged call from your ex-husband, but the rules are strict about when an inmate can use the phone." He shrugged and took off his hat to scratch his receding hairline. "Maybe someone else called you and just pretended to be your ex. You might want to think about other people who would like to see your hotel fail."

"I was married to Robert Flynn for six years. I think I'd know his voice." Lainie took the officer's card without glancing at it.

"Well, if you think of anything else, give me a call. We want to make sure the fire wasn't a deliberate act of violence." He tipped his hat and walked away to join another officer still talking to the fire chief.

Leaving Nico reeling from his words.

"Deliberate?" The word circled around and around his head like an obnoxious cartoon bubble. "They think somebody could have set the fire on purpose?"

Possibly to hurt Lainie?

The implications blasted through the confusing mix of emotions that had descended on him ever since he'd crawled into bed with her. No matter what else might be going on between them, he wasn't about to let anything happen to her.

"I think he just said they wanted to rule it out." She spoke with cool assurance, but her green gaze danced over the three-ring circus in the lobby as she bit her lip.

"I think we're going to make damn sure to keep you safe until they do." His father had drummed into all his sons' heads the importance of protecting the people around them. Especially women. And the old man didn't say that because he was a chauvinist. Giacomo Cesare had lost the love of his life and a baby daughter in childbirth and he'd grieved for them the rest of his life.

No, Nico couldn't blame his dad for thinking women were more vulnerable.

He waited for the inevitable bristling that would follow his words and was surprised when Lainie remained silent. He looked away from the coffee shop on the far side of the lobby, which seemed to be doing a great business despite—or maybe because of—the turmoil.

"Lainie?"

She stared off into space, her hand wedged inside her shoulder bag. He was surprised she'd managed to bring it with her since they'd left her suite in such a hurry.

"Are you okay?" He couldn't stop himself from putting an arm around her waist. "You want to sit down?"

She stiffened at his touch. Possibly because they weren't in a darkened room or rolling around in the privacy of her suite. "I'm fine. I just remembered something I probably should have shown to Officer Martinez."

Withdrawing a crumpled piece of paper from her purse, she moved through the crowd as if to hand it to him that minute.

Nico snatched it from her hand first, ignoring her

protest just because he was still tripped out over the possibility that someone might be trying to hurt her.

Guess your chef quit at an inopportune time. I sure hope it's not the first of many troubles to come.

"When did you get this?" The note might have been innocuous enough if it hadn't been combined with Flynn's call to the hotel after the explosion. "Is it your ex-husband's handwriting?"

"No." Her tone was brusque. Impatient. Scared? She yanked the paper out of his hand and folded it again. "I thought it looked like a woman's handwriting, but I wrote it off as someone being bitchy. Now that my kitchen has been blown up, however, I can't afford to overlook it."

"Damn straight you can't." He moved out of the way of the EMS team carrying the stand-in chef who'd been injured in the explosion. That could have been Lainie. Could *still* be her if he didn't watch her back and every other part of her until this whole mess could be sorted out. "And I'll tell you what else you can't overlook. Your safety is at risk here. You need to let somebody else manage things around here for a few days and get the hell out of Club Paradise until the police find out what's going on."

Her jaw dropped wide open. "Leave my hotel the week that Hollywood comes knocking?" She shook her head and stared at him as if he'd just arrived from another planet. "Nico, I wouldn't leave now if the lobby blew up around my ears. This hotel is my responsibility. My dream. And right at this moment in time, it just so happens to be my whole life."

She stared after the injured chef, concern etched in her eyes.

"I take it that's a no?" Did she have to be so stubborn? Still, he found it difficult to be angry with a woman whose mouth was still swollen from his kisses. A woman who was scared and trying hard not to show it.

Distracted, she didn't even answer. "I need to go check on that woman and extend an apology before I discuss the note with the police officer. Would you please excuse me?"

"If you won't do the smart thing and take a few days off, then I'm going to make it my business to watch out for you." He wasn't budging on that much. "In fact, I'm going to be your new best friend and roommate."

"I really don't think that's necessary." She edged away from him as the crowd in the lobby started thinning out. Firefighters taped off the corridor leading toward the kitchen and the last of the injured people— all members of the wait staff—were brought outside to the ambulance. "And I need to take care of about twenty different things right now."

"You won't be able to take care of jack shit if *you're* the one on the paramedic's gurney next time." Frustration churned through him. He tugged her closer just to grab her attention—not because he needed to touch her. Or so he told himself. "Someone's trying to hurt you. At the very least, they want to make trouble for you. The kind of trouble that could damn well get you killed if you're not careful. Is good publicity really more important to you than your life?"

She opened her mouth as if to argue, then clamped it shut again. Her jaw tightened. "If I agree to let you be my roomie for a few days, will you let me get back to work?''

His fingers loosened on her upper arms, then smoothed over the skin bared by the formfitting red dress she wore.

"Definitely. But I'm only leaving your side long enough to get things underway in the other kitchen and find some sucker to oversee the lobster prep. Then I'm stuck to your side and you're not going to shake me again until the police either have someone in custody or a damn good explanation for what's going on here.''

A handful of Lainie's West Coast guests breezed into the lobby from the street, shopping bags and cell phones in hand. They took in the turmoil in the smoky hotel, eyes wide. And if Nico didn't miss his guess, Bram Hawthorne was sneaking into the hotel behind them, a wide-brimmed straw hat and sunglasses almost disguising him.

Nico could feel Lainie straining to go play hostess and smooth over the mess.

"Fine." She nodded impatiently but at least she didn't argue. "Knock yourself out and don't forget to bring your own toothbrush. But I have to go."

She huffed away, calling him five different names under her breath. But all the names were familiar enough and they wouldn't stop him from watching out for her.

In fact, the sooner he organized the kitchen for the lobsterfest on the deck tonight, the faster he could be back at Lainie's side making sure she was well protected. He knew he could do the job.

He just wondered who was going to protect him from her.

9

SAINTS PROTECT HIM.

Bram held his breath as a foursome of bikini-clad tourists approached him. He didn't need to be mobbed right now in the wake of a serious accident at the hotel. No doubt the management would try to downplay the whole thing and it sure wouldn't help their cause if there were photos of him signing autographs in front of the wreckage.

Breathing a sigh of relief as the girls walked right on by him, he had to laugh. Who would have ever thought the Mississippi backwoods farm boy would see the day when he'd hope women wouldn't notice him? Unbelievable.

Tugging his hat down lower on his head, he dodged the big guy with the mermaid tattoo he'd nearly knocked over yesterday as he wove through the dispersing crowd in the lobby. He tried to remember where the movie's VIP lounge was set up so he could snag some dinner in peace. He remembered you were supposed to turn right at the statue of a naked Venus and left at the painting of a red poppy flower that looked exactly like a woman's genitals, but after that…

Daisy Stephenson popped into view, her sexy-as-hell body leaning up against a bookcase full of miniature erotic statues. She was scribbling in a small notebook with an orange pen.

Thank you, God. He plastered on his best grin just in time to see her scurry away in the other direction.

"Hey! Daisy, wait up." He double-timed it up the hallway, wondering when was the last time he'd had to chase down a woman before.

She turned, but she didn't exactly look ready to smile and flirt the way she had when they'd met earlier.

He whipped off his sunglasses and his hat. "I looked for you when the movie filming was over, but you were out of there so fast I didn't have the chance to talk to you."

After sliding her pen into the spiral of her notepad, she tucked the paper under one arm. "I figured I didn't need to stick around since I got the message loud and clear at the filming."

"What message?" He'd only sent her one that he knew of, and that was his request to visit the set.

"Obviously you wanted me to see the chemistry between you and Rosaria." She tossed her head as if to clear her long, wispy bangs from her eyes. They fell right back into place, one blond hank of hair curling around her wide blue eyes in a perfect frame. "You don't need to spell it out for me."

"Me and Rosaria? Hell yeah, I think I do need to spell it out for you. I don't have any chemistry with her."

Daisy huffed a rather inelegant snort that under other circumstances would have made him smile. "Could have fooled me."

"That was acting. And you know the only reason I did it so well?" Just remembering all his salacious thoughts about her was making him crazy to have her, to see if his wild imagination came anywhere close to the reality of being with her. Maybe because he had such a damn good imagination, too often he'd been disappointed when confronted with the object of his daydreams.

He didn't want it to be like that with her.

She shook her head, her blue eyes looking a little less certain. "Why?"

"Because I was imagining she was you the whole time." Footsteps in the corridor behind them made him remember where they were. He nudged her into an open meeting room nearby and shut the door behind them.

"You were?" She didn't protest when he took her notepad and laid it down on one of the tables set with coffee cups, legal pads and pens bearing the Club Paradise logo. He flung his hat and sunglasses aside.

"Yeah. I was." He stepped closer, intrigued by her willingness to give him the cold shoulder before. The fans who had chased him in the past had made it clear they didn't care what he did with other women, an attitude that had never set well with him and his more traditional values. "That's why I wanted you there during the filming. So I could—you know—get motivated."

Her blue eyes widened with surprise. Then narrowed with feminine wile. "I'll bet I could motivate you even more with a little incentive."

"Could you now?" His hands itched to cop a feel of those spectacular breasts inching near, but he would maintain the role of gentleman at least until she made her interest plain.

"Absolutely. And I have a feeling I would love every minute of it." The breathy words whispered over him before her voice strengthened. Hardened. "But I have to say I've been scammed by men in the past who are only after one thing. A girl can't be too careful, you know.''

"I've got gentleman written all over me." He thumped his chest and wondered if she'd heard about his reputation as a Hollywood nice guy. "How can I make you trust me?"

She shrugged. "Hmm. I dunno. But I did have a lot of fun at the movie filming until I thought you were trying to wave Rosaria in my face. Maybe I'd learn to trust you if we spent some more time together…maybe went to a few of the movie events with you?" She ran her fingers up his chest, hovered at the top button of his shirt and danced along the notch of bare skin above the button. "I'd love to give you some very explicit motivations for this sexy movie of yours."

"I can admire a woman who knows what she wants." Hell, any Hollywood female probably would have bargained for driving rights with the brand spanking new Mercedes SL55-AMG the *Diva's Last Dance* producer had given him as sort of an under-the-table signing bonus. "Why don't you consider yourself my personal VIP?"

"A VIP?" For a moment her blue eyes sparkled like a kid at a Christmas, but then she seemed to recover herself as she gave him a wide grin. "Perfect. I wouldn't mind showing a certain someone at Club Paradise that I'm not the low-level peon she thinks I am." Daisy stood taller in her superhigh heels, which still only put her at his chin.

Sex in exchange for what sounded like Daisy's revenge. An unholy bargain if ever he'd heard one.

"You're on."

The smile she flashed had him so dazzled he almost

needed his shades back on. ''Killer. You want to go back to your room?''

She almost looked as eager to be alone as he was. Tempting. Oh so damn tempting.

But despite his carnal bargain with Daisy, he hadn't been raised to take advantage of women—even the kind who seemed to know how to watch out for themselves.

''And shirk my duties as your VIP host?'' He tucked her hand inside his arm and scooped up her notepad along with his hat and sunglasses. ''Not on your life. First I'm going to get you dinner in the VIP lounge and then I'm going to give you a tour of the movie-making process.''

Daisy blinked. Once. Twice. Again. Had she heard him clearly? No sex until *after* he'd lived up to his end of the bargain? Holy moly. The man must be a saint.

Not that she thought she was such a hot piece of ass and he should be dying to go to bed with her. But in her experience, once men knew sex was even a remote possibility, they hounded a woman—any woman—until they got what they wanted. For Bram, a movie star who could have sex whenever, wherever and with whomever he chose, to feel compelled to uphold his end of the deal first…well, that was just plain unheard of.

Also, it was just plain nice.

Daisy hurried to keep up with him as he guided her out of the meeting room and down another hallway toward the lounge. His bicep felt deliciously warm and solid as he steered her along and, once they got into bed, she vowed to knock his socks off as a thank-you.

In the meantime, she crossed her fingers Lainie Reynolds would make a pass through the VIP lounge while Daisy was with Bram. She didn't know why it mattered so much that she thumb her nose at the woman who'd fired her. The woman whose respect she'd once coveted. It might be petty and small-minded to want to rub Lainie's nose in her mistake, but that didn't stop Daisy from hoping she and Bram would be seen together.

And while she was at it, she also hoped Bram wouldn't have any reason to open her notebook. As a high-school dropout who'd struggled to earn her G.E.D, Daisy might not be the world's best educated woman, but it didn't take a genius to realize a nice guy like Bram would be disappointed to read what she had written there.

CRISIS AVERTED.

Lainie patted herself on the back as she savored her last bite of lobster doused in warm butter. Moonlight danced on the ocean in watery time to a swing tune delivered by a local big band she'd called in to play at the impromptu lobsterfest. With the backdrop of the sky and stars, she could almost forget her hotel was still crawling with cops and two outside cleaning crews. While South Beach singles whirled to the music and indulged themselves at the extra tiki bars erected for the occasion, Lainie thanked her lucky stars she'd managed to divert attention from the explosion and show her guests a good time.

At least for tonight.

"Are you going to finish that?" Nico leaned closer, her ever vigilant chaperone since they'd struck their deal. He'd pointed to a half a lobster tail on her plate while they sat on cushions in the sand around a low table lit with flickering torches to ward off the dark.

"Maybe." She pulled her plate near in a ridiculous urge to protect whatever she could from this man determined to invade every facet of her life. "There's probably more to be had if you ask one of the waiters."

"Want me to feed you?" He reached for her plate, ignoring all her defensive posturing. "You can pretend I'm your love slave and force me to feed you with my fingers. Doesn't that sound like a potential theme for one of your exotic shindigs?"

She stabbed the remaining shellfish with her fork before he could steal it. "Sounds like a fun theme, but I'd rather feed myself tonight."

Shoving his cushion back from the table, Nico leaned back in the sand to stare at her. "You're still mad at me for forcing my way into a few nights in The Diva Penthouse with you, aren't you?"

"Mad? No. Inconvenienced? Terribly." She shoved her plate aside and signaled to the waiter to clear their end of the low, makeshift table. Everyone else they'd been seated with was long gone to dance and mingle or roast mini dessert fare over the open flame of a beach bonfire.

"I can't believe you." He shook his head, his dark hair just grazing along the edge of a crisp white collar he'd left open at the neck. The man looked damn good in torchlight, even if she happened to be frustrated as hell with him right now.

"What's so hard to believe? That I'd rather go about my business without a two-hundred-pound shadow lurking over my shoulder every second of the day when even the police—whose *business* it is to protect people—didn't seem overly concerned about the coincidence of one bitchy note and a kitchen explosion in the same week?"

And she didn't even mention that, despite his willingness to help, Nico could also be a bit pushy about his opinions around the hotel. In the course of the few hours it took to set up the party, Nico had weighed in on at least fifty percent of the decisions she'd made—how to set up the tables, which band to contract, how late the party should run, what to tell the media about the explosion, what to say to the film crew about the ordeal. She'd have her hair all torn out by tomorrow at this rate.

He dug in his pocket and somehow she wasn't surprised to see his Hacky Sack make a reappearance. Did he carry that damn thing with him everywhere?

After three tosses and catches, his gaze narrowed. "Is that what's really bothering you? The fact that I want to make sure you don't get blown off the planet by another Club Paradise crisis? Or are you just mad because you gave in and slept with me?"

The waiter who had been clearing the table made a sound like he'd swallowed a lobster whole. Lainie gave him a glare that sent him fleeing for cover, dishes in hand.

"How kind of you to inform my staff of our one-time brainless decision to be intimate." Yet even as she bit out the angry words, she couldn't help but think how intimate they'd been. How Nico had taken her to sexual places she'd only read about. She drummed her fingers on the table and looked out over the sea, searching for patience. Tact. "Honestly, maybe I am mad I slept with you."

For once, he didn't say anything, but she could hear the rhythmic toss and catch of the small beanbag, a sound that soothed her as much as the steady roll of the ocean waves.

"Maybe I've been trying to keep men at a distance by holding onto my bitterness toward my ex." Heaven knew, she hadn't made any effort to date over the past year. "Because as long as I didn't let anybody too close, I couldn't get burned again. And whether or not that approach was shortsighted is beside the point. It was really working for me."

"Was it?" He leaned forward, slapping the Hacky Sack on the table as he moved closer. His white shirt gaped open as he leaned, giving her an inviting view of lean male muscles and bronze skin. "Can you really say you were happy living and working in your own world, isolating yourself in The Diva Penthouse like an ice queen and not coming out except to coerce your staff into compliance with your wishes?"

She couldn't have been more surprised if he'd tossed his wine in her face. The calm roll of the waves mocked the stormy torrent of her emotions. "You make me sound like a heartless witch. Is that how you view me?"

Was that how other people viewed her?

"Hell no. I think you're a kick-butt CEO with a thriving business on her hands. And maybe you've had to be a little tough and demanding while you were getting things off the ground, but the good news is, Club Paradise is a huge success." He reached to touch her hair, to smooth one palm over the straight strands and down to her shoulder. "I just think maybe you've been operating at code red for so long you don't know how to step back and loosen the reins."

His words stung. And not just because she feared there might be a strain of truth in them. Mostly they hurt because he'd felt the need to point out her flaws. She squeezed her temples in an attempt to hide a tear that was highly uncharacteristic of her. "Well, thanks very much for those astute insights. I'll certainly keep them in mind the next time I hire out one of those touchy-feely management-training services to put me in better touch with my employees. Remind me not to bother being honest with you the next time you ask a nosy question."

She tried to rise to leave, but he had plenty of time to stop her since they were sitting on cushions on the sand. She only made it to her knees when he hauled her back down. Stiffening, she counted backward from ten to prevent herself from yelling. Focused on the last of the police cruisers finally pulling away from the hotel.

"Shit. I'm sorry." He held her tight while he apologized. Loosened his grip just a little once the words were out. "Sometimes I let my mouth get away from me. Okay, all the time I let my mouth get away from me. It's one of the less endearing qualities that's hereditary in my family. I had no right to critique how you run your hotel."

"Or my staff?"

"Or your staff." He let go of her completely, giving her the option of leaving now if she wanted.

Oddly, she didn't want to. They sat on the beach and watched the incoming tide from the relative comfort of their seat cushions for a few moments before she spoke again.

"I know I've been a demanding boss this year, but I have eased up since our numbers started nudging into the black." She knew she couldn't be a perfectionist with every aspect of the hotel. That's why she'd hired middle managers—to motivate their employees and be responsive to their needs.

She didn't know why it mattered that Nico understand her perspective, but it did. They'd shared something special when she'd brought him back to her suite, and he deserved at least to see where she was coming from.

Nico knew he shouldn't touch her. Had refrained wherever possible all day since he didn't plan on letting things get out of hand between them again. But his fingers found their way to the skinny spaghetti strap of her long white knit dress, his thumb tracing the path between her collarbone and the narrow piece of fabric.

"The only reason I said anything is because I think we're alike in that way. I was a pretty demanding coach this year because the Panthers were in the division finals. I couldn't afford to slack off and be the nice guy. But I told myself that in other years, when we weren't in a position to win, I wouldn't have to work my players so hard."

"And you figure I'm not in a play-off position now, so I ought to step back?"

"Again, it's your business not mine, but I thought as long as Club Paradise is doing so well maybe you could afford a few days off." He hesitated. "Maybe you could give people like Daisy the fake waitress a break."

She rolled her eyes. "Daisy and I have more issues than what you see on the surface. She tried to suck the tonsils right out of Brianne's fiancé last fall. And while I realize it's none of my business if she wants to throw herself at unsuspecting men, I didn't appreciate paying her salary as a cigarette girl while she wandered around the hotel on a search-and-seduce mission."

"It seems like she's successfully snagged Bram's eye." Nico nodded toward the pair dancing in the sand a few yards away. They must have ditched the dance floor for a more private beachside clinch.

Lainie peered over her shoulder at them. ''Bully for her. Maybe I'll get lucky and she'll start impersonating his maid instead of his waitress and she can finally pay me back some of the lost work hours she owes me.''

''Damn. Forget what I said before. You're way tougher on people than me.'' He liked the way she tilted her head to the side when he touched her. As if she wanted him to touch more.

She looked softer tonight in her white dress, her cheeks pink from the fresh air and from a glass of merlot. Her legs were crossed at the ankles, the straps of her gold sandals wrapping around her feet and up her legs to tie in a long bow.

''I have very high standards.'' Her gaze followed Bram and Daisy.

He didn't say anything, turning over that piece of information in his mind.

''And before you make any remarks about my high standards leading me to marry a criminal, let me just say that, on the surface, Robert Flynn looked like everything I wanted in a man.''

''I wasn't going to say anything of the sort.'' He was an impulsive speaker and occasionally insensitive, but even he knew better than to bring up the ex. ''But please, go on. I think I'd like to hear what Lainie Reynolds wants in a man.''

''Wanted. Past tense.'' Shifting on her cushion, she waved away the maintenance man who'd come to break down their table. The rest of the dinner tables had been moved inside for the night, but they continued to sit at theirs, their torch burning low while the rest of the party picked up speed around them. ''But back then, I wanted stability in a man and I wanted a great outward appearance. Not necessarily a GQ-looking guy, but a man who knew how to behave in public situations and could hold his own in a media interview since my career was already putting me in the spotlight."

"And from what I remember," Nico mused, "Flynn was great with the media. There had even been some talk of him running for a political office a few years back."

"He ate up the limelight. Part of the reason why I thought we'd be a great match." She flipped her hair over one shoulder, her red nails a stark contrast to her fair hair and white dress. "I'll be the first to admit I chose him for rather superficial reasons, but I meant it when I said in sickness and in health and all that do or die stuff. Marriage meant forever as far as I was concerned."

He processed this new information about Lainie. He hadn't expected someone so bitter about her divorce to be such a proponent of wedded bliss.

"Unless, of course, your husband turns out to be a major criminal who steals from you, cheats on you and asks his mistress to run away with him to the Cayman Islands. And then, forget it. I don't need a club over the head to realize some marriages just aren't meant to be."

"You deserved better." He wondered if she'd ever give any guy a chance to show her better.

"At least it's over." She made a sweeping gesture with her hands as if she was shoving the whole mess away. "I avoided personal bankruptcy, and I found a way to turn this albatross of a hotel into the hottest destination on the strip."

"What about marriage?" Maybe if he heard her rail against the very idea, he'd be able to stifle this connection he felt with her. Because, bottom line, he was a family guy. Perhaps if he could get it into his head that Lainie would never share those same values, they could get back to attraction, pure and simple. No, strings sex seemed to be something they could both be very comfortable with.

"Marriage? Ha!" Her disparaging expression confirmed all he needed to know. "It'll be a cold day in hell before I walk down a church aisle again."

He could feel the connection between them fade. He could never go for a woman who wasn't as family oriented as he was. The sting of disappointment surprised him more than he would have expected over a woman he hardly knew. Why should he care if she wanted something totally different out of life than he did?

He should be cheering because now he could at least simplify things and just enjoy having sex with her. Memories of their afternoon together, never far at bay today, blasted back into his brain. Lainie teasing him, tormenting him, going wild...

Her voice broke through his fantasies. "But then again, one day I'll want to have kids. Hard to believe that I could want a baby and not really care about a husband, but somehow I always pictured myself as a mom one day."

And just like that, all of Nico's fantasies shifted. Changed. Incorporated wild sex with Lainie that one day resulted in kids. The ultimate dream of a highly sexed, family-oriented guy.

Just like that, his sense of connection to her was back, stronger and more dangerous than ever. Because as much as he might deceive himself into thinking he could have those things with Lainie, the reality of the situation was that it would be a cold day in hell before she walked down the aisle again.

For that matter, he didn't even know what he wanted to do with his life now that his hockey career was over.

As the encroaching tide grazed his toes and the moon rose higher in the sky, Nico promised himself not to get any more tangled up with a woman he didn't stand a chance with. Despite the great fantasies, it looked as if he'd be in for a cold night alone.

10

DAISY KNEW SHE HAD TO BE dreaming because enchanted nights like this only happened in Disney movies or magazine spreads.

Soft sand cushioned her feet as she danced with Bram in the moonlight on their own little stretch of beach. A thick carpet of stars shone above them, making her deliciously dizzy every time her partner bent her backward for a dip. Like now.

Bram slanted forward, lean muscles taut as he positioned an arm underneath her back, his hips inches away from hers. They stared at one another, breath coming fast, while the rest of the seaside partygoers faded into the background. The horns of a seventies disco tune couldn't compete with the steady roll of ocean waves at their feet or the fast thrum of eager heartbeats.

Bram Hawthorne was so much more than she'd expected. So much better than she'd imagined.

And she hadn't even gotten him naked yet.

As of today, Daisy knew she'd been going about the whole dating process all wrong. But then, where would she have learned how to relate to mature, marvelous men like this?

Her mother had been convinced Daisy's stripper's body would be enough to snag a great—read: rich—husband and had counseled her daughter not to give away her favors to any man who didn't pack a fat bottom line. And after seeing a few of his daughter's uninspired report cards in junior high, Daisy's father had advised her to focus on finding a husband in high school rather than trying to get into college.

Great advice, Dad.

Of course, she couldn't blame all her problems on her highly dysfunctional family. That's why she was getting the hell out of Dodge this fall after saving her nickels from a hodgepodge of crappy jobs over the past few years. She just hadn't counted on meeting a man who would make her long for impossible things.

"So tell me, how am I doing with the VIP treatment?" He drew her upright again, but his feet slowed as their song faded and a dance beat took over the club's outdoor sound system. "Are you feeling very important yet?"

More than he could ever guess. But she wouldn't let on that a guy she'd known for a day had been more kind to her, more respectful, than anyone she'd ever known. He'd think she was big-time screwed up.

"You've outdone yourself." She said it with her flirtiest smile, a surefire way to make her words sound less serious. "You let me eat dinner with you in the VIP lounge. I got to tour around South Beach in your Mercedes. And then I got to parade through this elegant, schmoozy party and dance ten feet away from my ex-boss who thinks I'm a half-wit. Yeah, I'm feeling pretty important by now."

Bram looked over her shoulder toward the place Lainie and some hot-to-trot athlete were still seated. Bram's trademark silvery eyes darted back toward Daisy.

"Why do you care what anyone thinks about you? You don't need her approval."

"No, but—" Despite the sexy, all-woman dress she'd chosen from the ridiculously overpriced hotel boutique earlier, she felt awkward all of a sudden. Would her behavior appear immature to someone like Bram? "I guess I want it anyhow."

Turning, she peered beyond a cluster of torches and a small banquet table still heaped with hors d'oeuvres toward Lainie and the guy who seemed to be glued to her lately. "I mean, look at her. She's so damn together even when her hotel blows up around her ears and her chef quits."

The woman seemed practically indestructible.

"It's a talent to make the best of a bad situation," Bram agreed, leading her to the banquet table. He reached for a handful of strawberries dipped in dark chocolate and offered one to Daisy while he downed two himself. "I hear the police are investigating the explosion to see if it might have been set deliberately."

Bram reached for more strawberries and wondered why Daisy seemed pale all of a sudden.

"Are you okay?" He led her to a pile of abandoned beach cushions the maintenance guys had cleared away after the seaside lobster supper. Digging a few of them out and brushing them off, Bram settled Daisy on one and dropped down close beside her. "You look a little nervous."

She patted her purse, a shiny sequined bag she'd haggled over for ten minutes with the boutique owner before agreeing on a price. Then, as if taking comfort from knowing her bag was still at her side, some of the tension slid out of her shoulders.

"I'm fine. Just surprised anyone would make trouble

for the hotel since it's the hottest thing going in town this year. Even the competing nightclubs and resorts appreciate its success. After all, it brings more people to the beach to patronize everything else down here.'' She drew her legs up underneath the long hem of her silky blue dress.

Bram tried not to stare, but he'd been hypnotized by that outfit of hers all night. The fabric followed every curve of her body.

''Maybe they'll find out it was just an accident.'' He wondered how much longer he should wait before he asked her to come back to his room. Five minutes? Another hour?

He'd barely survived dancing with her without jumping her. But then, he'd been fantasizing about her way too much during his scene with Rosaria earlier in the day. Normally, he wouldn't even let his brain tread down that path with a woman he'd just met, but with Daisy he had to plead extenuating circumstances.

He needed a distraction, any distraction, before he blurted out something really stupid and blew his chances with her altogether. ''Can I ask you a question, Daisy?''

His mind scrambled for a topic while she looked at him with her wide blue eyes. The soft light of the torches made her skin glow with warm color. She brushed white sand off her toes, her pink toenails peeking out of silver sandals.

''Hmm?'' She leaned closer, bringing her lush mouth almost within kissing distance.

It was all he could do not to touch his lips to hers, but he knew one brush of their mouths would touch off more fireworks than a populated beach could handle.

"What have you got against the lady hotel manager?"

"What?" She started back, blinking.

Okay, so maybe it hadn't been the smoothest segue, but lust-ridden men weren't known for their ability to think clearly. He pointed toward the sleek blonde dressed in a simple white dress. "Nico Cesare's new girlfriend. She's your former boss, right?"

"I haven't got anything against her." Her voice cracked a bit.

Every actor worth his salt knew that was a quick way to convey a lie on stage. But before he could wonder why she'd bother to fib, she shook her head.

"Maybe that's not true. Actually, I guess I resent her just a little because she fired me from the classiest job I ever had. I loved working here. Being a cigarette girl might not sound overly glamorous to a movie star, but to me—"

"Are you kidding? Who wouldn't want to work here? They call it Club Paradise for a damn good reason." He stared out to the water and wondered what it would be like to have a boat. To sail into that endless blue without five million other worries. "Would you look at this view? Shoot, I'd wash windows here if it meant I got to hang out on the beach now and then."

"Please. You're one of the hottest stars in Hollywood. I don't think you'd trade that for washing windows."

"The money's good. But it's not always all it's cracked up to be. There's not much free time once you've got a face people recognize. Fans can be great, but they also want a piece of you—your time, your smile, your T-shirt... Sometimes it's nice to get away from that and just be anonymous."

As soon as he said it, he realized he sounded like a total ingrate. He was damn lucky to have caught so many breaks in his career.

"I don't mean to come across as some spoiled-brat actor. I'm just not very good at protecting my time."

"You don't sound spoiled. You sound like a really nice, normal guy who just happens to be a movie star." She brushed her hand over her evening bag, flipping all the sequins first in one direction, then in the other. He imagined those soft, small hands of hers on his back, on his chest, touching him with those same slow, hypnotic movements. "You want to go for a walk down the beach?"

He wondered if it was too soon to make his move. "Actually, I have some lines I need to run through tonight before I go to bed. Would you want to come inside and read through them with me?"

It was true enough. He just hadn't mentioned that after reading a few lines he planned to kiss her right out of that body-conscious blue dress of hers. Or so he hoped.

She surprised him by hesitating. Had she changed her mind about their bargain?

"Okay." She nodded slowly, her hand still tightly gripping her purse. "Maybe just for a little while."

Bram managed not to lick his chops as he extended a hand and helped her up from their cushions. Surely he could ease any worries she had and talk her into spending the night.

Especially since he had a particularly juicy scene in mind for them to rehearse. With any luck, he'd be able to move right from fantasy to reality and they'd walk away with a night neither of them would ever forget.

"JUST SO THERE'S NO CONFUSION going into the bedroom, there's not a chance in hell I can sleep with you now, Lainie." Nico's latest pronouncement seemed to be just another attempt to push all her buttons as he followed her through the hotel later that night.

"You are *so* getting on my nerves, you know that?" Lainie tried to play it cool, but the fact was she'd been stressing big-time ever since the police had told her to watch her back and Nico had steamrolled her into letting him stay in with her.

Then their shared confidences at the beach had only confused things, tightened the knots inside her all the more. What had she been thinking when she told him she wanted to have kids one day? She had a business to run, a hideous track record with marriage and no plans to put herself through the hell of divorce again. What made her think she could ever have any kind of family? And worse, why had she felt the need to share something so personal with a guy like Nico?

Obviously, the explosion had rattled her far more than she'd realized.

Wanting to make sure he hadn't misunderstood her earlier, she smiled at him over one shoulder. "Who said I wanted to sleep with you anyway?"

She did, of course, but she wouldn't admit it. Or, to be more accurate, every nerve ending in her way too turned on body wanted to sleep with him. Her head had known all along it was a bad idea.

Tromping up the hallway toward The Diva Penthouse with slightly shaky legs, she didn't stop at the door to her usual suite.

"Come on. After the mind-blowing sex we had earlier, you mean to tell me you don't want a rematch just to see if we can top that?" He stared at the labels on the hotel-room doors. "Hey, wait a minute. Isn't your suite back there?"

"We're not staying in my suite." Too small. Too tempting. Too many memories of her tearing off her clothes in her haste to get busy with this man. "Since you're with me, I figured we might as well snag one of the vacant two-bedroom suites."

"A two-bedroom suite?" He came to a halt behind her while she used her master key card on the door to the Roman Retreat. "You mean you didn't plan on sleeping with me, either?"

If he intended to take her mind off the explosion, his plan was definitely working. She smothered a wry laugh. "Let me get this straight. You already knew you wouldn't go to bed with me, but you're somehow offended that I had no intentions of going to bed with you?"

"Damn straight." He nodded, scowling.

"That makes no sense." She shoved her way inside the suite, desperate to escape Nico and his hot body. His sexy dark eyes. The bronze skin of his chest that made her fingers itch to touch him....

"It makes perfect sense. I had a very good reason not to hit the sheets with you—" He whistled low as he followed her into the Roman Retreat. "Wow. Cool digs."

Tossing her purse and the key on the granite countertop of the small kitchenette, Lainie welcomed the change of topic and the momentary reprieve from her thoughts of jumping him. "It was partially inspired by some of your sister's photos of Italy. Summer saw the pictures and loved the ancient architecture and the aged patina of the buildings in those pictures, so she used some of that in the decor. She also threw some of that infamous Roman decadence into the mix.''

Lainie glanced around the room with appreciative eyes, more able to enjoy the room Giselle had helped design now that the two of them had healed their old rift. A smooth cobblestone path wound through the whole suite, connecting rooms that were otherwise tiled or carpeted. The walls were varying shades of white, as were the furnishings. Eggshell-colored sheer silk curtains lined walls already painted a creamy off-white. The silk was gathered with gold cord at intervals to expose intricate murals of ancient Rome painted on the walls.

But the best part was the abundance of small Persian rugs on the floors, the gold cushions strewn on the smattering of chairs and wooden benches, the low wet bar that housed a seemingly endless supply of wine and grapes.

''Is there really food in here?'' Nico moved toward the bar built into a rolling cart that could be easily passed around the room so that lounging guests didn't need to walk across the suite in order to indulge.

''Don't tell me you're hungry after all that lobster.'' She'd eaten every bite she could manage. ''Dinner was fantastic, by the way. Thank you for lending your cooking expertise to haul us through another meal.''

She watched him prowl around the suite, his strong, athletic thighs straining the fabric of his dark trousers ever so slightly. And the view from behind...so fine.

''I'm not sure the lobsterfest can uphold the restaurant's reputation since that great review Giselle got last month, but at least the guests enjoyed it.'' He rattled the lock on the minibar. ''You know how to break into this?''

''The master key is on the kitchen counter.'' She would have retrieved it for him, but she didn't trust herself to walk past him. She settled onto one of the low cushioned benches in the living area, telling herself she'd only sit for a minute before she retreated to her room. Her home-free zone.

''Got it.'' He sprinted back from the kitchen so fast she would have missed him if she blinked. ''Athletes burn a lot of calories, you know. If I want to be in shape by the time the season rolls around again, I need to keep up my strength. Practice starts in less than two months.''

''Heaven forbid I deny you your second truckload of food.'' Kicking off her shoes, she made herself comfortable as she watched Nico drag a bunch of deep purple grapes from the refrigerated section of the bar.

He popped grapes in his mouth at high speed, maintaining a steady train of fruit with one hand while he opened a bottle of wine with the other. Digging deeper in the refrigerator he found a wheel of cheese and slapped it on top of the bar. Crackers followed.

She took an odd pleasure from observing him. And not just for the obvious reasons. When she'd married Robert she'd nurtured secret hopes of being just a tiny bit domestic together. Of hanging out in pj's and watching the late show or maybe one day foraging for food after the kids went to sleep.

Goofy, romantic stuff.

Robert hadn't been interested in sharing meals with her unless they were out in public, in which case he'd been superattentive. But at home he was even more driven than she, opting to spend all his free time massaging business deals and far-flung professional contacts. Possibly with other crooks, she thought now.

Whenever she and Robert did go out to dinner, they'd usually end up meeting Summer and her old boyfriend, Paul Bertoldi, who'd once managed the hotel's restaurant. Lainie had struck up a friendship with Summer because of many shared plates of tiramisu while Robert and Paul talked business.

No, Robert hadn't been much for hanging out. But somehow Lainie could picture Nico watching the late show and eating pretzels in bed.

"This is great stuff." He inhaled one piece of cheese as he sliced some more. "You need to get The Diva Penthouse done up like this one and enjoy the high life."

"It's *not* The Diva Penthouse. But maybe one of these days I'll get it updated." She didn't know why she'd been putting it off. Or maybe she did. "I guess if my room is renovated then there's no excuse for me to live at the hotel any longer. I'd just be taking up rentable space. And frankly, I'm too busy to house hunt right now."

"You don't have your own place?" After arranging some cheese and grapes on two plates, he kept one for himself and rolled the cocktail cart over to where Lainie sat. He followed more slowly, lowering himself to the floor near her seat, his back resting alongside her legs.

She shook her head and resisted the urge to run the arch of her foot up his bicep. "Robert maxed out the home equity loan to give himself more spending cash when he skipped town. I gave up the whole thing to the bank and moved in here while I got my accounts in order."

"And I thought *my* finances sucked. At least I've got no one to blame but myself for the position I'm in.

I just need to sell some of the toys I've acquired to loosen up the cash flow.'' He wolfed down a few more crackers and brushed the crumbs off his shirt.

Definitely the pretzels-in-bed type.

''Were you able to save any money while you were playing?'' Not that she had any right to ask. ''Actually, scratch that since it's so completely not my business.''

She stuffed a grape in her mouth before she said too much, reminding herself that she couldn't afford to feel too comfortable around him. Still, she found herself savoring the grape juice knowing Nico's kiss would taste the same way.

''I invested some of it, thank God. There's not much I can touch since it's all tied up, but with any luck, it's working for me so that I'll have a few bucks in my pocket down the road.'' He poured two glasses of wine and passed one to her. ''My old man used to take us to Italy every year and I don't have a clue how he afforded it, but it was the coolest thing we did as a family.''

''Really? My family went to the local swimming hole for a picnic twice each summer. Same thing— highlight of my year.'' Her mom had usually gone home with a different guy each time, but at least she'd made an attempt to be there. Lainie's grandfather had done all the real work of packing picnic baskets and frying chicken. He'd been her rock growing up.

''Lainie Reynolds at a swimming hole?'' His grin showcased more teeth than a dental commercial. ''Did you have all those red fingernails and designer shoes back then? I'm trying like hell to picture this but I'm coming up dry.''

''I don't think I'd discovered the merits of red polish until law school. Back then I was still pilfering what-

ever my mom happened to have on her nightstand.''
She nibbled a few bites of cheese and missed Kentucky
for just a few seconds.

"Do you ever go back?"

"My grandfather died last year and he was my only
real connection to the place. My mother…well, she and
I don't have much of anything in common."

"I'll bet you intimidate her." His hand moved to
her ankle. Skimmed over her bare leg for the briefest
of moments before he moved away again.

The imprint of his fingers remained, her skin mourning the loss of his touch. She gulped her vintage merlot
like a shot of cheap Kentucky bourbon and reminded
herself they weren't going to sleep together tonight.

"And just what makes you say that, when you've
never even met my mother?" Though she had to admit,
it might not be such a bad guess. As Lainie had grown
older she'd learned to see her mother's behavior with
more mature eyes. And she had wondered if her mother
wrestled with self-esteem issues that went far deeper
than Lainie's own insecurities.

Maybe her divorce made her more sympathetic to
what man trouble could do to a woman.

He rolled his eyes. "You intimidate everyone." Tipping the bottle of wine toward his glass, he refilled his
cup and moved the container toward her. "More
wine?"

She moved her glass away. "Actually, I think I need
to learn moderation around you, but thanks anyway.
And I don't intimidate everyone."

"Ha. You forget I've been keeping my eye on you
for the last month." His stare made her feel short of
breath.

What little wine she'd had was starting to feel warm

in her veins. Either that, or the thought of Nico watching her all the time was making her hot and bothered. She let her gaze roll over him, his tall, athletic body half sprawled at her feet. His crisp white shirt at odds with his easy manner that could turn fierce with just a little provocation.

"Oh no." He edged away from her a few inches.

"What?"

"Don't look at me like that." Swigging the rest of his drink, he stared back, his dark eyes never leaving hers.

"Like what?"

"As if you're remembering everything that happened between us out on your balcony today. In detail."

"Arrogant man." She smoothed a hand over her hair and lied through her teeth. "I wasn't thinking any such thing."

"Like hell." Rising, he shoved aside the remnants of his late-night snack and backed away. "Listen, I've got to go find a bed where I can lie awake and think about you without having the option of touching you. Can you tell me where you want me to sleep before I start compromising those damn boundaries of yours left and right?"

Disappointment curled through her as she moved to her feet.

"You can have either bedroom." *And you don't have to sleep alone.* She didn't say it, but she sure thought as much. "You know, I didn't mean to get on your case about looking out for me today." The conciliatory words stuck in her throat just a little. "For the record, I appreciate all the help you've given me."

He stopped his backward shuffle toward the bedroom

door, his feet rooted to the spot on the decorative cobblestone path. Looking down at the floor for a long minute, he finally wrenched his gaze up to meet hers, shaking his head.

"I want to be over there by you so badly right now." He shoved his hands in his pockets, fingers knotted into fists.

She licked her lips, wishing they could go back to sex for the fun of it. But somehow he'd moved beyond that, had decided things were getting too serious between them.

And damn it, she'd just been starting to really appreciate the idea of having fun.

"But I can't. We can't." He leaned into the door frame. "I know I said that I could handle a rebound relationship, but being with you today made me realize I was lying."

Lainie gripped the back of a nearby chair and squeezed it until she feared she'd snap the wooden frame.

"Lying?" Her head spun with the ghosts of her past. All of Robert's lies. She fought to conjure any words that might make it sound as if she didn't care, but came up blank.

"Yeah. I realized I can't keep things simple or superficial. It's just not in me." He pounded the door frame of the smaller bedroom with his fist. Once. Twice. "I can't afford to sleep with you, Lainie, because I'm already starting to care about you."

And as if that hadn't shocked her right off her high heels enough, Nico disappeared into the bedroom and shut the door behind him.

She might have pursued the matter if she could have convinced herself all she wanted was the sex. The heat.

But as her disappointment turned into an all-out sting, she realized that, despite her best efforts, she'd come to care about him just a little bit, too.

And the notion rocked her world every bit as much as today's explosion.

11

ALONE AND LONELY and really resentful of the fact an hour later, Lainie stared at the closed door to Nico's room and wondered how she'd ever get through the night.

The late news on the plasma wall screen depressed her. The snacks from the minibar didn't taste good without someone to share them with. She was debating going to bed when a soft knock sounded at the hallway door.

Should she wake Nico?

Tiptoeing to the door first, she peered through the glass peephole and found a mass of platinum curls sprinkled with clip-on pink braids.

"Summer!" She flung open the door, grateful for the unexpected company.

"Hi there." Dressed in a shimmery turquoise dress with a strand of colorful crystals around her neck, Summer held a trayful of decadent desserts, the same kind of sample tray one of the restaurants downstairs used to show off that night's sweet-tooth offerings. "I found a few leftover desserts in the kitchen. I don't think Death by Chocolate goes bad after two days, do you?"

"Definitely not." Mouth already watering, Lainie helped Summer balance the tray, prettily decorated with flower petals and a lit pink votive candle, as she made her way inside. "But how did you know where to find me?"

"I tried your suite, and when you weren't there, I called the front desk to ask if you'd moved to another room." Summer frowned as she settled her offering on a cocktail table. "I kept getting a really unsettling vibe about you tonight. I know you think my intuition is a crock, but can you deny that you needed a friend tonight?"

"Well…that is…no." Lainie peered over her shoulder at the closed door where Nico slept. "Nico and I seem to be communicating at cross-purposes."

Summer plunked down on the carpet to sit beside the food. "I knew I needed to bring chocolate. When there's man trouble afoot, chocolate always helps." Shuffling aside a dish of crème brûlée, she snagged the Death by Chocolate plate and handed Lainie a fork. "You like this guy?"

Settling on the floor alongside her, Lainie decided just this once her need for a confidante outweighed her desire to be seen as a woman who had it all together. "I can't believe you're eating junk food again. Haven't you been on a health-food kick all year?"

"I still am." Summer reached for the flourless chocolate cake drizzled in raspberry sauce. "Which is why I'm opting for the dessert with a nutritional fruit serving. But no fair changing the subject. Do you like Nico?"

Lainie stabbed a forkful of seven-layered heaven and munched a fortifying bite. Girl talks had never come naturally to a woman who liked to maintain a certain facade of business capability. Especially girl talks with someone as whimsical as Summer.

But times were tough considering Lainie was sleeping alone tonight. Maybe she needed a little feminine wisdom to help her figure out what to do next.

"I like him," she admitted, unable to deny the truth to herself any longer. "Don't ask me why, because I don't understand it, either. He's very he-man traditional and he doesn't respect personal boundaries at all. He's very opinionated and in-my-face when I'm accustomed to keeping guys at a distance." Not that she wanted another relationship like she'd had with Robert. Far from it.

She'd known early on that they didn't connect on any deep level, but she'd been okay with that because she was insecure about a lot of things in her past. She'd never found a way to reconcile her Kentucky roots with who she had become.

"Sometimes it's good to have someone push your boundaries. If Jackson hadn't completely ignored mine, I'd still be a rootless wanderer with no clue what I was looking for. I thought I wanted a tattooed surfer who was as unconventional as me, when what I really needed was a straitlaced politician." She grinned as her eyes turned dreamy. "Well, sort of straitlaced. Did I ever tell you he was sporting a tattoo all along? He just put it somewhere that isn't immediately obvious."

Clearing her throat, Lainie reached for one of the bottles of water on the serving tray. She wasn't about to discuss Jackson Taggart's tattoos. "But what made you realize Jackson was the one? How did you know he was right for you and Paul Bertoldi wasn't? And please don't tell me it was intuitive, because you know damn well I don't have any crystals or sixth sense, okay?"

"Oh yeah?" She jerked a thumb toward the minia-ture coffee service complete with coffee filters, tea bags and mugs. "I could always read your tea leaves and tell you whether or not Nico is right for you."

"Not funny."

"Okay. Honestly? My first clue was Jackson's sense of honor. He kind of tricked me into meeting him in the first place, but he came clean about it as soon as I confronted him with it, and he offered to leave right away. Paul had a sneaky, underhanded side and he wouldn't have admitted to it if you threatened to singe his favorite tattoo."

"Nico's painfully honest," Lainie admitted, wondering if seven-layer chocolate cake had seven times as many calories as plain old devil's food or, if by some cruel dieting math, it had seventeen times as many calories. "I've never met a man who says whatever he thinks. You know, I don't think it even occurs to him to censor himself."

"Sounds like the ideal man for a woman divorced from one of Miami's most notorious liars." Summer set aside her half-eaten dessert and toyed with one of the crystals around her neck. "And as for the cake, don't worry about it. Calories don't count when you're dishing about men. It's an unwritten rule you'll grow to appreciate as we initiate you into the rites of girl talk."

Lainie nearly dropped her plate. "Don't even tell me you just read my mind." Had she been thinking anything really incriminating about Nico? Like how much she wanted to crawl into bed with him later?

"Okay then. It was just a guess because you were studying your next bite so intently." Summer glanced at her watch and stood. "I'd better get back home since Jackson is catching a late flight from a meeting he had in Orlando today. And for the record, I think Nico seems like a great guy. He gave Giselle a hard time about working here because he was really protective of her, but it was always obvious he adored her.''

Lainie's cheeks turned warm. What could she say to that?

After clearing their dishes and picking up the tray, Summer moved toward the door, taking all her bright colors and funky intuition with her. ''I'd never tell you what to do, but maybe it couldn't hurt to get to know him better before writing him off as all wrong for you. He might be more right than you ever expected.''

Hurrying to open the door for her, Lainie realized she'd just survived a girl talk complete with chocolate and dishing about men. And it hadn't been goofy or silly. It had been fun.

''Thanks, Summer.''

''My pleasure. And if you change your mind about the tea leaves—''

''I know who to see.'' Smiling, Lainie promised herself she'd try to do what Summer suggested and get to know Nico a little better. Find out more about him.

Then she could decide if she wanted to distance herself from him altogether, or if she'd put all her energy into making sure he never shut her out of his bedroom again.

THE HOTEL DOOR LOCKED automatically behind them as Daisy entered Bram's room with him. Tamping down an attack of nerves, she told herself she wasn't worried about being alone with Bram in the Harem Suite.

''Come on in.'' Bram wandered deeper into the room toward a stereo tucked into a walnut-colored bookshelf. "What are you in the mood for—jazz? Pop? You name it."

Would she be showing her roots too much if she asked for Lynard Skynard? Of course she would. Bram didn't strike her as the beer-in-a-can, Southern-rock type.

"Anything is fine." She smiled and hoped he didn't think she was about as interesting as milktoast. She had zero experience being a good girl, but with this decent, nice guy, she really wanted to try.

"This suite is gorgeous." She'd heard rumors about the decadent hotel room at Club Paradise, having never actually seen it, since she got fired before the rooms were all refurbished. She knew this suite was booked up to a year in advance because of its fantasy appeal. And although she'd tried to tell herself the room was probably so popular because of its high sex factor, like the Fun & Games Chamber, she had to admit once she saw it that it was also just plain beautiful.

White silk and satin draped everything from the bed to the walls to an elegant chaise. Gossamer-thin curtains surrounded the bed, the fabric gathered and tied back with purple silk. Heavy wood furnishings and dark rattan baskets grounded the prevalence of white, while richly colored Persian rugs provided color and texture. Eastern-inspired, jewel-tone lanterns hung from the ceiling on dark metal chains, casting colorful patterns throughout the white room.

Daisy could see herself whipping off her dress for an impromptu belly dance if she wasn't careful. What better setting to show off her belly button piercing? But she refused to be a Miss Fast and Easy tonight.

"It's a little too uptown for me," Bram admitted, his quicksilver eyes taking in the elegant surroundings as an old reggae tune drifted through the speakers. "Every time I come up from the beach I feel like I'm adding another few pounds of sand to the carpet, but it's definitely easy on the eyes." He gave her a wolfish grin. "Come to think of it, you fit right in here."

Tempting as it might be to trade sexy lines with a major superstar, Daisy bit her tongue. "Thank you." How was that for demure? Still, knowing she wouldn't be able to make demure conversation for more than ten seconds, she changed the subject. "You said you wanted to rehearse tonight?"

"Yes." Nodding slowly, Bram seemed to be taking stock of her low-key demeanor. "I'll go grab an extra copy of the script."

Maybe he was used to having women jump him as soon as they were alone with him, but she would not be that woman.

Watching him walk away, Daisy patted herself on the back for her ability to redirect. She still couldn't believe she—Daisy Stephenson, the high-school dropout with the bad-girl reputation—was a guest in Bram Hawthorne's hotel room. Obviously, some sort of celestial miracle had taken place to line up so many stars over her bottle-blond head.

As he disappeared into an adjoining room, Daisy told herself all she had to do now was get through the script reading without drooling on him and she would have undisputed proof that she could be a nice girl.

In the other room, Bram had no clue what happened to the flirty waitress he'd met this morning, but she'd somehow morphed into a more reserved, sweet female he barely recognized. What happened to the bad girl? Had he read her wrong this morning when she'd been smiling and leaning so close that her impressive breasts had loomed inches from his cheek?

No. She was probably just waiting for him to make a move. A piece of cake now that he had the *Diva's Last Dance* script in hand. If she showed the least little sign of being resistant, of course, he'd abort the whole mission faster than an agent dropped a fading movie star. Not in a million years would he upset Daisy. Besides, those good-old-boy manners the press swooned over weren't just for show. He was a Southern gentleman, damn it, even if he was keeping a big part of his life secret from her along with the rest of the world.

He ducked out of the small parlor area and waved the papers as he ambled closer.

Eyes moving over Daisy and her slightly stiff posture, he remembered that some women liked guys to make the first move. In practice, he always found it easier to wait for a woman to show interest in him first. But given that Daisy was the woman he wanted—unpretentious, down to earth, non-silicone-enhanced—then he'd make his move and hope like hell he hadn't read her wrong earlier today.

Handing her his copy of the script, he pointed out the scene he'd be filming tomorrow with Rosaria.

"It starts off as a dance scene." He wouldn't tell her where it ended up. "And it would help if we could dance our way through it so I could get a feel for the blocking."

Taking the pages as reverently as if they were a holy text, Daisy read over the first few lines of setting and nodded. Then frowned. "So dance with you while I read?"

Yes, ma'am. He couldn't wait to touch her again, to feel her in his arms. He didn't know what he'd done to chase away her flirty side, but he would do his damnedest to bring it back.

"Yes. That way I get a better feel for my positioning while I'm talking." He held out his arms to her. Waited. "If you can just feed me the heroine's lines, it will help me make sure I know my own."

Stepping into his arms, she looped her own around his neck, still clutching her script to read over his shoulder. Her soft, clean scent drifted about him—honeysuckle, maybe. Or some other unassuming flower that flourished in the heat.

His hands moved to her waist, situating themselves as low as possible on that seductive curve without being too forward. He pressed her close, covertly feeling through the thin fabric of her dress for any hint of panty lines.

He felt only soft curves.

And got a hard-on in two seconds flat.

"How should we dance?" She looked up at him with wide blue eyes as she shifted in his arms. "Does it matter?"

He knew what dance they should be doing right now, but he bit his tongue to keep himself from spelling it out.

"Lady's choice," he managed finally, keeping his hips just far enough away from hers. "Why don't you make the call?"

"Won't you have to do this a certain way tomorrow?" She bit her lip as she read over his shoulder as if seeking the answers in the script.

"We have a little creative license with this kind of thing." He lifted his hand to cup her chin, to turn her gaze toward his. "What do you think, Daisy?"

"Two-step." Her breath came in shallow puffs, as

if she could feel the same heavy heat between them that he did. "Do you L.A. boys know how to two-step or am I going to have to teach you?"

The hint of challenge in her voice brought a smile to his face. Damn but he liked it when she flirted with him.

"Don't forget I'm a Mississippi boy underneath the thin veneer of city polish." He tightened his hold on her waist with one hand and untangled her free arm from about his neck with the other. Weaving their fingers together, he held her close and waited for her cue.

She could plaster herself against him for the kiss he was dying to taste, or she could read the first line he'd marked in the script. He held his breath, hoping like hell for the former, knowing even the latter would earn that kiss eventually.

If he could only be patient.

"Are you sure you know what you're doing?" Her words came from the script, but they seemed to mirror her thoughts.

Picking his moment, he began the simple steps of a dance every kid in his town knew by the time they were in kindergarten. Hell, his high-school prom had been a barn dance, so he remembered a thing or two about two-stepping.

"Lady, I know exactly what I'm doing." The confidence of his CIA agent character gave Bram the green light to move his hands up Daisy's back to the patch of bare skin above her zipper. "You just follow me and I'll take care of you."

"Then do you care to tell me why we're wasting time dancing?" Daisy's eyes widened as she read her line.

His grip tightened on her reflexively as he slowed

his step. He drew her hips to his, molded her breasts against his chest. "You call this wasting time?"

"I call it a poor substitute for what we'd both rather be doing." Her voice trembled a little on the line, her eyes were full of blue flames when he met her gaze.

"Never let it be said I cheated you out of what you really wanted." He halted in the middle of the Harem Suite, more than ready to follow through on the act the script called for next and hoping Daisy wouldn't mind.

His mouth descended to hers, his lips brushing across hers softly at first, then with a determination he couldn't suppress. She tasted like toothpaste and marshmallows from the beach bonfire.

If he'd been worried about her rejecting him, his fears evaporated as she dropped the script on the floor and wrapped both arms around him with surprising strength.

Her breasts flattened against him, the taut peaks teasing his chest right through her silky blue dress. The uninhibited response was exactly what he'd hoped for and better than he'd imagined.

He was already calculating how many steps away they were from the bed when she broke their kiss.

"You maneuvered me into this by having me read that scene, didn't you?" She looked surprised. Shocked.

Ah damn.

He loosened his grip, hoping he hadn't screwed things up. "I'm sorry, Daisy. I guess I hoped once we started reading, it might, you know, inspire us."

He waited for the feminine outrage. Already imagined their pictures on the cover of the *Enquirer* after Daisy sold them her story.

Movie star seduction technique backfires!

But Daisy surprised him with a wicked grin. "Turns out you're not always such a nice guy after all, are you?"

And that was a good thing?

He shrugged, not letting go of this woman without a fight. "I really wanted us to be together tonight."

Suddenly her hands were all over him, down his back, up his chest, hovering over his shoulders.

"Trust me, I like that you've got a bad streak in you, Hawthorne." She pressed her hips against a raging erection and wiggled. "It makes me feel better about my own."

Oh yeah. "Please say that means you're going to spend the night with me." He wanted to be sure he was interpreting all the signals right before he lost himself in Daisy's honeysuckle scent.

"I'm staying." Her fingers combed through his hair while he inched the zipper of her dress lower. "And you can be *my* audience for a change."

"Consider me captivated." He paused on her zipper to slide out of his dress shirt. When he reached for her again, she danced back, out of his reach.

"How can you be captivated when you haven't seen anything yet?" With a swish of her hips she turned on him and glanced back at him over one shoulder.

"Hell, I'm more than ready for the show." He put two fingers in his mouth and let out a wolf whistle. "Take it off, sugar," he drawled, his gaze pinned to her half-unzipped dress for any hint of her breasts.

She sashayed around him in a bump and grind that set all the right parts to jiggling and would have put any roadhouse stripper to shame. The sexy slow music he'd put on earlier didn't deter her in the least. If anything, she just made her movements that much more tantalizing to match the beat.

"What do you think, hotshot?" She taunted him as she cinched her dress up high, but not quite high enough. "You like what you see?"

"I'm loving what I see, but you must know I want more."

"Maybe I do, too." She nodded toward his pants still belted around his hips. "And I think I'd be more inclined to give you what you want if you show me something in return."

He reached for his belt. "If this is part of the bad streak you've got, I think I'm going to like it." Easing his zipper down, he was only too happy to oblige Daisy's demands.

Her gaze cut to his trousers. "I think I'm going to like this, too, Mr. Hawthorne. Why don't you tell me what you want to see first?"

His mouth dried up just looking at her, the straps of her dress already falling off her shoulders, her shag haircut giving her a permanently tousled look.

He stepped closer to run one fingertip over the generous curves of her cleavage. "I want to see these."

"Tell you what," she whispered as she reached for her hem. "Why don't I just give you the whole show at once?"

Whipping her dress away in a swirl of blue silk, she was suddenly standing there mouthwateringly naked in front of him. Pale and perfect, she cupped her breasts in her hands as if in offering while a rosy pink stone glittered from the indent of her belly button.

He muttered an oath, or perhaps it had been worshipful praise. Either way, he was on top of her in an instant.

Hands exploring, seeking, finding where she liked to be touched best. Mouth licking, tasting, inhaling her. They rolled to the floor as one, the exotic bed forgotten in their haste to be horizontal. Bram tugged off his pants to press himself into her thigh, the slight pressure of her cool skin not nearly enough to take the edge off his hunger for her.

He vowed he'd find a dozen ways to make her come later, if he could only just get inside her this first time. Hauling her over him, he tugged one of her slender thighs on each side of his waist. Positioned the damp heat of her over his straining cock.

She threw her head back as she rode the ridge of him, her slick warmth beckoning him inside.

He nearly lost his mind, could have forgotten all about protection if she hadn't suddenly scrambled off him.

"I've got condoms in my purse. I think. I hope." She rifled through the contents of her tiny sequined bag and then squealed as she withdrew a red circle that looked like a coin. "Never fear, latex is here."

He had a condom somewhere in his room, but he mentally blessed Daisy for having kept enough wits about her to be careful.

She knelt over him, taking his cock into her mouth and clamping her lips about him so sweetly he had to tug her aside. Her unrepentant grin told him she knew exactly what she'd been doing as she rolled the condom over him and straddled his hips.

Hello, beautiful.

The view from the floor was incredible, but he flipped her to her back just the same, needing some more control this first time. He steadied her hips with his hands, his fingers sinking into soft feminine flesh at the same time he buried himself between her thighs.

Daisy's body arched, her breasts lifting high off the floor in an invitation he couldn't ignore. He drew one peaked nipple into his mouth while he tweaked the other between his fingers. Suckling and kissing her, he played with her breasts as his hips found the rhythms she liked best.

Finally, she cried out his name on a moan, her fingernails digging deep into his shoulders while her body pulsed wildly around him. He didn't have a chance of holding back his own release. His hand moved to her belly where the pink stud scraped against his thumb. His fingers curved around her hip, holding her there as the shudders of his release wracked through him. Again and again.

It had been way too long since he'd done more than flirt with a woman.

When he pried open his eyes that had somehow drifted shut, he found Daisy smiling up at him.

"That was something." She said it with just the right note of awe in her voice, as if being with him was the best time she'd ever had in bed. Or on a floor. "Bet you can't do that again."

He would have laughed if he could have found the energy. Instead, he settled for drawing her into the crook of his arm. He kissed the top of her head and wondered how long it would take to uncover all her bad-girl secrets.

"I bet you're dead wrong."

BETTER TO BE DEAD than sexually unfulfilled.

Or so it seemed to Nico two days later as he slapped a puck across the ice so hard it ricocheted off the boards and sailed up into the stands. He'd spent the past two nights alone in the most hedonistic bedroom he could imagine while the woman he wanted slept on the other side of a Sheetrock wall he could have easily put his fist through.

All in all, a piss-poor way to relax.

Skating across the ice in a low-budget rink he'd built downtown a few years ago to give city kids a place to practice, Nico stared up at the clock protected by iron bars. In another half hour he could retrieve Lainie from the police station where he'd dropped her earlier. She hadn't received any more notes, but there had been a couple of crank phone calls that made the police more wary.

Robert Flynn was now being kept under closer watch at the prison, and the cops were kicking up the investigation a notch. They wanted a list from Lainie of any potential enemies, disgruntled employees and former employees who might have taken out their frustration by torching her kitchen. He'd been surprised when he'd caught a glimpse of her long list, but according to her, you didn't get ahead in business without pissing off a few people. Still, she seemed exceptionally good at the pissing off part.

Did it make him a sucker that he kind of liked that about her? Other women he'd dated had been occasionally put off by his tendency to be aggressive when it came to getting what he wanted and expressing his views. But next to Lainie, he was simply holding his own. She was every bit as strong willed and opinionated as he was, possibly even more so.

It only followed that they'd argued about going to the police station together. She hadn't wanted him there, insisted she'd be well protected in a cop shop, but he hadn't budged on at least driving her there and back.

He might not be able to sleep with her for fear he'd fall for her in a big way. But that didn't mean he wasn't going to follow through on his promise to look out for her until the police found out who was behind the explosion. His money was still on the smarmy ex-husband who must have plenty of connections outside his jail cell.

Plus, Lainie's list had included one of Flynn's old Rat Pack cronies at the hotel who hadn't been caught yet, as well as the slew of employees she'd churned through in a short amount of time. Even pseudowaitress Daisy Stephenson with her big blue eyes and crush on Bram Hawthorne had been on the list. Though he could not imagine why a girl like Daisy who had caught the eye of a superstar would be wasting time setting off explosives.

Nico skated to the edge of the ice and slipped the rubber guards on his blades to walk to the locker room. Maybe he ought to head back to the station early so he could put his two cents in with the police. He'd probably put a hell of a lot more thought into what was happening at Club Paradise than any overbooked civil servant.

He'd almost made it to the safety of the locker room when a peewee skating class plowed out of the dressing area, their pads and helmets making them bounce off each other in their scramble to take the ice. The littlest kid at the end of the pack took an elbow to the chest and fell face first on the rubber mat lining the concrete floor.

"Hey, bud, you okay?" Nico scooped him up under the arms, setting the kid's skates back on the mat.

When the rug rat wearing a Panthers jersey looked up at him, he realized the kid in question was a green-eyed little girl, her brown braid tucked into her big hockey sweater.

"You're Nico Cesare." She whispered the words with a flattering amount of wonder before she belted out a yell that stopped the rest of her class in their tracks. "Hey, everybody, it's Nico Cesare!"

So much for giving the cops his informed opinions. He was effectively captured, surrounded by screaming kids in less than ten seconds.

LAINIE WATCHED THE KIDS swarm Nico from behind a fat pole near the bleachers and smothered a laugh. She'd fudged the time she needed to be picked up at the police station so she could drop by the ice rink early and see him in his element.

Not that she was slowly growing obsessed with the man or anything. She simply wanted to get an idea of who Nico Cesare was outside of his dedication to his sister. Obviously, he was much more than that to these kids who all jammed papers and pencils and hockey cards in his face for autographs.

She snickered again as he glanced up at the clock and then back down at the sea of excited little faces all talking at once. Perhaps she'd laughed a bit too loud because his head whipped around in her direction, as if he had ultrasensitive radar where she was concerned.

"You." He pointed an accusing pink pencil with a fat teddy-bear-shaped eraser in her direction. "What are you doing here?"

He kept the menace out of his tone, but she saw the frustration in his dark brown eyes.

"Don't worry. I had a squad car drop me off out

front when I finished up early.'' No need to admit she'd planned as much so she could get a sneak peek at the arena he'd built in this working-class section of downtown Miami. She'd bared enough of herself to Nico yesterday without admitting her growing fascination with him. How many men would not sleep with a woman because they cared about her?

Unorthodox male behavior certainly, but intriguing just the same. Every time Lainie thought about Nico caring about her she experienced a juvenile bout of butterflies.

Like now, for instance. Two days of backing off and getting to know Nico better had only convinced her she would be insane not to talk him back into her bed. They could keep things simple and still like each other. It didn't have to turn into a Relationship with a capital R.

''A squad car dropped you off?'' He looked slightly appeased as he handed the teddy-bear pencil back to a padded and helmeted little hockey player who had to be a girl. ''Did an officer walk you inside?''

''No.'' She strutted closer to where he stood, infusing her stride with just a little more hip action than usual. ''But he definitely watched me walk all the way into the building.''

Nico snorted as he patted another kid on the helmet and picked up a piece of paper to sign. ''I'll just bet he did.''

''Are you disappointed you've got no reason to be mad at me now?'' She peered around the small ice rink, wondering where all the parents for these kids were hiding. A teenager with a whistle who was probably the coach watched a Zamboni finish cleaning off the ice.

"What makes you think I want to be mad at you?" Nico spoke to her while he nodded to a kid who was showing off a hockey stick with a red-and-gold Panthers logo on the handle. He gave the boy a thumbs-up and then proceeded to sign his stick.

The teenage coach blew the whistle then, and the pack of kids backed off reluctantly until Nico encouraged them to practice so they could have their turn in the NHL one day.

Did he have to be so damn good with kids? Robert had only cooed over babies when it made a good photo op.

"Lainie?" He took off his skates and tossed them into a big sport bag. His hockey sweater followed, leaving him clad in a red-and-gold Panthers T-shirt and black track pants. He stuffed his feet into sneakers and stared back at her. "What makes you think I'd *want* to be mad?"

She shook her head to clear it of visions of Nico and kids. For all she knew, he was only nice to kids when it suited him, too, right? Wrong. She didn't trust her gut about men for a lot of reasons, but she trusted that what she'd just seen hadn't been fake.

"I don't know. Guess I figured maybe it would be easier for you to keep your distance if you could stay angry." She hugged herself as she walked with him toward the exit, her breath a visible puff in the chilly air. She hadn't realized how frigid it would be around an ice rink, her long silk skirt and close-fitting blouse providing zero warmth.

"Being angry won't help. I'm pretty damn sure I could be mad at you and want you at the same time. In fact, after the hell of the past two days, I think I'm going to want you no matter what." He shoved open a set of double doors and held one for her as she stepped outside.

Now her butterflies picked up speed, her pulse quickened and her legs grew liquid.

"Did it ever occur to you that it might be hideously unfair for you to make all the decisions about whether or not we sleep together?" Did he think the past two days had been a walk in the park for her? Besides, he was the one who'd talked her into sex in the first place with his whole assurance that it was just a rebound thing. Why did he get to back out after he'd convinced her? "Why don't *I* get a say?"

He stopped cold, his black hockey bag banging against his thigh. "We both get a say. But unless we agree, we can't do a damn thing about what we want."

Like hell. If she'd accepted that kind of attitude in life, she'd still be barefoot in a Kentucky hill town and taking over the family bourbon business.

"Then I'll just have to get you to agree with me on this one, won't I?" She paused, waiting for him to join her on the trek toward his shiny black pickup truck. "I'm a divorcée who's been without sex for over a year, Cesare. I'm willing to go to bat for my next orgasm."

12

NICO WAS STILL REELING three hours later. Lainie hadn't said another word about any potential plans for seduction on their circuitous route home, but he knew how driven and determined she could be. If she was coming after him, then, by God, he'd have a hell of a time keeping his pants on.

Now, as he pulled into a parking space on Ocean Drive near Club Paradise, he wondered with a mixture of anticipation and fear how soon she'd start her campaign.

"Thanks for running errands with me." Lainie scooped up her handbag and shoved open the truck door before he could help her. "I'm sure you had better ways of spending your day than waiting around while I schmoozed my newspaper contacts."

It hadn't been a hardship to watch her schmooze. Well, except for her chat with one of the business editors who kept stealing surreptitious glances at her legs. "Not a problem."

"Holy crap." Lainie halted in her tracks on the sidewalk outside the hotel. Her silk skirt swung around her legs with interrupted momentum.

Nico followed her gaze to the two police cruisers with flashing lights parked in front of the property. His protective instincts went on high alert. "You shouldn't even be here."

"It's okay. The building is still standing, isn't it? That means there weren't any more explosions." She took another step toward the Mediterranean-inspired building.

He caught up with her a few yards from the entrance, thinking to himself that there still could have been an accident, a robbery, a fight, or worse. But he didn't share that with Lainie who already looked a shade paler despite the steely set to her delicate jaw. She'd probably be charging into the damn building even if it was burning down.

Dragging open one of the oversize front doors, Nico ignored his good manners and let himself in the building first. If there was trouble brewing, he'd be the one to scope it out.

All his worst-case scenario fears hadn't prepared him for what he spied once they were inside.

Daisy, the pretend waitress, was sandwiched between two police officers, her slender wrists in handcuffs. Her hair was tousled and she'd traded last night's fancy evening dress for a pair of shorts and T-shirt bearing a UCLA logo.

Bram Hawthorne was standing between the trio and the door as if determined not to let the group walk by him. He gestured wildly with his arms as he talked, his usual Southern charm looking as frazzled as his bed-rumpled hair, wrinkled T-shirt and cargo pants. Photographers already circled the scene, flashbulbs popping nonstop to capture every moment on film.

"This is an all-new style of explosion," Nico muttered under his breath, but Lainie was already in motion, her heels clicking a determined beat across the polished marble floor.

Damn.

His feet stepped double time to catch up, something he seemed to do a lot around this woman.

"What is the meaning of this?" She kept her voice low, her question directed to the same two police officers who had investigated yesterday's kitchen mishap.

"We talked to the chef who quit two days ago and found out Miss Stephenson had instigated some strife among the employees in the kitchen, including an attempt to talk the former chef out of her job."

"Surely you aren't arresting her for being mouthy." Lainie raised one blond eyebrow, a skeptical expression that seemed to go hand in hand with being an attorney. "Anything else?"

Bram answered first. "Ms. Reynolds, I'm sure this is all a big mistake."

Nico noticed Daisy's eyes cut to the movie star, her lip trembling ever so slightly.

"Forget it, Bram," she whispered, loud enough for everyone but the reporters to hear. "This kind of scandal isn't good for you or the movie."

He threaded his fingers through his spiky hair, making the mop stick up even higher.

"Quiet." Lainie shot them both a quelling look before turning her attention back to the police. "Officers? Does this woman have some sort of connection to the explosion yesterday?"

She damn well better not. Nico hadn't thought Lainie treated the other woman too nicely, but that didn't give this Daisy person any right to risk lives.

To risk Lainie's life.

"After the chef fingered her, we took a ride out here to question her. She gave us permission to search her handbag and we found incriminating evidence in the form of a 'to do' list with ways to bring you low."

The round-faced cop waved the paper under Lainie's nose.

Even as she snagged it for a read, Lainie rolled her eyes at Daisy. "You gave them *permission?*"

"They made it sound like I had no choice." She glared at the police officers, who didn't appear too concerned. "And I tried to tell them that someone else could have seen my list because I never would have put it loose in my purse the way they found it. I always keep stuff like that in a little pocket binder with my notepaper and my other lists—ways to make a million in five years, new ways to cook pasta with low fat sauces…that kind of thing."

"And ways to make trouble in Paradise?" Nico peered over Lainie's shoulder and read the list.

Creating trouble in Club Paradise:
1. Initiate personnel problems among the staff.
2. Lay the groundwork for an explosive situation.
3. Publicize the whole mess on network television, or better yet—a full-length feature film.
4. Force The Diva—ice princess Lainie Reynolds—to remember my name.

Anger churned inside him. "She could have killed someone."

Lainie passed the note back to the officer. "You'll compare the handwriting to the other note I received?"

Bram faltered in his pacing. "There are more?"

Nico imagined it must suck to suspect your new girlfriend of sabotage, deceit and God only knows what else.

The lady cop nodded toward her partner and gave him some sort of sign to prod the other guy toward the door. "We really can't discuss the investigation with any of you. Ms. Reynolds, we may need you to come back in for further questioning."

Lainie was already pulling a card out of her purse and stuffing it into the officer's hand. "This is Ms. Stephenson's lawyer. Daisy, when you contact him, just let him know I've referred you and, for God's sake, don't say another word until your attorney is present."

Daisy's jaw dropped open moments before her eyes narrowed. Confusion, suspicion and a healthy dose of fear were all reflected in her wide blue eyes. Was it such a surprise that Lainie would lend someone a legal hand? She'd practiced law for six years before trying her hand as a businesswoman, for crying out loud.

"Damn." Nico hadn't realized he'd spoken until Lainie stared at him while the police were taking Daisy away. He shrugged. "She sure doesn't look like a would-be killer."

The photographers followed Daisy and the police, leaving Bram alone for a few moments. He muttered a string of curses before he scowled at Nico. "I'm sure she didn't do a damn thing." He stuffed his hands in his wrinkled pants as he looked at Lainie. "You don't think she did, either, do you?"

Lainie's hands didn't look particularly steady as she stuffed a leather card case back in her purse. "I don't know what to think, but I can tell you that Daisy's handwriting doesn't match the note I received, and it doesn't account for why my ex-husband is harassing me." She gave him a tight smile. "Then again, it could simply be a case of me having way too many enemies to count."

Without thinking, Nico slid his arm around her

waist. Felt her trembling even though he couldn't see it as he stared down at her.

"Why don't we go upstairs so you can unwind? Kick your shoes off and think this through?" As soon as he suggested it, he knew she'd never go for it. The woman had independence and determination down to some sort of twisted art form. "Or we could go check out whatever they're filming today for *Diva's Last Dance*."

Movies made great distractions for women who were in too much trouble and the men who cared too much about them. Jesus. If he wasn't careful, he'd be forming his own freaking self-help group in no time.

"Shit." Bram looked down at his watch. "I don't know if we're going to be filming squat today. How the hell can I run a love scene when my—" His gaze moved back to the glass doors leading outside where they were putting Daisy in a squad car. "I might have to ask for a delay."

"No." Lainie hitched her purse higher on her shoulder, grabbed Bram's hand and gave it a quick squeeze. "I'm telling you, Daisy couldn't be in better hands than my former legal partner's. She'll probably be back in the hotel by nightfall."

Nico had his doubts about that. Even if she was released on bail, wouldn't she have to stay away from Lainie, the woman she obviously detested?

"You think so?" Bram stuffed his hands in his pockets as he looked at Lainie with hope in his eyes, his heart practically hanging off his sleeve and bleeding right there on the hotel floor where he'd been pacing.

Poor sucker.

Nico vowed he wouldn't get trampled like that again. No way. No how. It wasn't a pretty sight.

"If not, I'll arrange private, quiet transportation for you to head down there tonight. I know plenty of people in the Dade county jail system who can bend a few rules for me." Lainie smiled at Bram. "Especially if there's an autograph in it for them."

Bram seemed to settle down. Deep breaths slowed his pacing. "You think I should do the scene?"

"Put all that adrenaline to good use and give a killer performance. Trust me, you're not going to be able to do a thing to help Daisy until after she's talked to the police on her own. If anything, you'll only draw a hell of a lot of attention to her case and she'll be all over the news as a suspected arsonist simply because you're there with her. She won't be able to go to the grocery store without six people recognizing her as Bram Hawthorne's jailbird girlfriend."

Bram swore, shook his head, but finally nodded. "You're right. What else do I have to do right now anyway?" He took a few steps backward. "We're filming in the Fun & Games Chamber again if you want to come up. Rosaria loves an audience." He rolled his eyes and then pivoted, jogging through the lobby toward the elevator, weaving his way through the slowly dispersing crowd.

Nico blinked, trying to make sense of what the hell just happened. His arm still slung around Lainie even though her slight tremors had ceased, he shook his head.

"I don't get it."

"What?"

"The cops arrest one of your least favorite people and you rush to her defense."

"I did no such—"

"You give her access to somebody that I'd be willing to bet is one of the city's best attorneys, and then you play Susie Make Peace with Bram by helping him heal his trampled heart.'' Nico didn't understand a damn thing about women, but he'd thought he'd at least gotten a handle on hard-nosed Lainie Reynolds. Until now.

Lainie still stared across the lobby in the direction Bram had gone. ''Do you believe a nice guy like him went for a bad girl like Daisy?''

He stood a little taller. ''I think nice guys get sucked in by bad girls all the time. Just look at me and you. It's all that stuff about opposites attracting.''

Sighing, she stepped closer to the self-service bar at the coffee shop off to one side of the lobby. ''Please. As much as I hate to say it, I have the feeling you and I were cut from the same cloth—bad to the bone.''

''Hey, speak for yourself. And you still haven't answered my question.'' He followed her toward the coffee counter as she pretended great interest in the java selection. Why did he get the feeling he'd just witnessed some of her lawyer ability to talk circles around people?

''Oh?'' She reached for a cup.

''Yeah, oh. What made you decide to be so nice to Daisy when she's obviously gunning for you?''

Sighing, she helped herself to a latte and waved to a teenager manning the register. ''Honestly? I thought over what you said about me giving Daisy a hard time and I guess I realized I did bust her butt too much.''

Surprised, he grabbed a cup for himself and filled it with ice water, always a good countermeasure to have on hand whenever he was near Lainie.

''You thought about something *I* said?''

''Yes. And when I took it to the next level and asked

myself why I gave her such grief, I realized it was because she reminded me of my mother. No sense of self-esteem so she makes herself feel special by seducing a lot of guys.''

''Whoa. Hold up there.'' He sipped his ice water just to get his bearings. ''I think you covered a whole season's worth of *Oprah* in about two seconds.''

''It's neither here nor there anyway. But I realized I needed to cut Daisy some slack.'' Lainie waved away the words as if they didn't matter, when Nico knew damn well they did. Had she just admitted her mother was a...female player?

Somehow this new information helped Lainie's ramrod-straight posture and all-business manner make perfect sense. Maybe it also explained why she married a guy like Flynn who looked so upstanding on the outside. Damn but he was turning into Mr. Insightful lately.

Knowing she wouldn't appreciate any comments on what she'd just told him, Nico moved on. ''And what about my other question? You told me why you were nice to Daisy, but what made you decide to help out Bram? I thought for sure you'd encourage him to chase down his girl and skip the filming so that the movie crew would have to stay in South Beach that much longer.''

''I have a very good reason for wanting Bram to film his scene today.'' She glanced up at Nico over the rim of her latte, her green eyes sending a message that made him want to loosen his collar.

''What was that?''

''I thought it might be fun inspiration for us to watch a love scene together.'' She nodded toward the elevator with cool composure. "Are you ready to go upstairs to take in the show?"

"As if we need inspiration." Nico's hand clenched around the cup of water, not convinced that drinking it would help put out the fire she'd just ignited with only a handful of words. He might as well dump the drink down his shorts. "This is your way of tormenting me, isn't it?"

"I told you I was determined to wrangle a repeat performance from you, Cesare." That Mona Lisa smile of hers surfaced, a wicked light dancing in her eyes. "I figured you could use a little incentive before I take you back to my room tonight."

NEVER LET THEM SEE YOU SWEAT.

The advice of a long-ago law-school professor rang in Lainie's head as she bluffed her way through an admission that made her nervous and left her wide open for more rejection. But, damn it, she wanted another night with Nico even more than she wanted to maintain her diva persona.

The ice-queen facade had always helped her in business and had carried her through an emotionally tumultuous year, but it sure as hell hadn't been very effective at landing sexy dates.

Time to melt away some of that cool exterior so she could get what she really wanted. She just hoped she didn't overheat while she waited for his reply.

"You want to watch the hot scene with me?" Nico pressed his empty cup to his head after chugging the contents in one long swallow.

"That's right." Her latte rippled in its cup, thanks to her attack of nerves. She started walking toward the elevator, hoping the movement would hide the telltale signs of panic. Fear. God but she hated putting herself on the line in her personal life. "You don't have to go if you don't want to, but I'm watching the scene and since you've made it your mission to look after me, I figure you'll end up watching it, too."

The string of curses he reeled off behind her soothed her, giving her reason to hope he would be swayed by the steamy new movie sequence.

Fifteen minutes later they were taking their places in the Fun & Games Chamber for the filming. As Lainie glanced around at the half-dozen other guests standing behind the roped-off area, she couldn't help but wonder how Daisy was faring at the police station.

She seriously doubted the girl was behind the kitchen explosion. If anything, seeing Daisy's scrawled "to do" list had only succeeded in making Lainie realize how inaccessible she'd been to everyone around her for the last year. She'd never been a big touchy-feely type, but before her divorce she'd at least been able to maintain some friendships. Since then she'd been moving through life with a huge chip on her shoulder. The time had come to get over herself and move on.

Love sucked. End of story.

That didn't mean she had to take out her frustrations on cigarette girls who didn't take their jobs superseriously. And it didn't mean she needed to deny herself male companionship. Just because men could be painfully unfaithful didn't mean they had no value.

Take Nico for example.

Sneaking a glance sideways as the director gave last-minute instructions to Rosaria and Bram, Lainie's gaze lingered on the strong lines of Nico's face. Square, stubborn-as-hell jaw. High cheekbones. Crooked nose that reminded her he wasn't afraid to fight for what he wanted.

She admired him. Beyond the fact that she wanted desperately to jump his bones, she had to admit that she respected who he was—the kind of guy who looked out for his sister, the kind of guy who put family first.

The nervous flutter rippled through her again, making her think she'd be better off concentrating on the more simple, obvious appeal of the man. The white-hot sensual experience he could provide.

A feat which wouldn't be too difficult given that the director was calling for quiet on the set and the actors were taking their positions. She inched closer to him, shamelessly employing her body in her quest to seduce Nico.

"You're not fighting fair," he whispered in her ear as the director's slate snapped shut.

Her heart picked up speed at his proximity, his male warmth seeping through her dress to heat her skin beneath. Stretching up on her toes, she whispered back.

"So send me to the penalty box. You're welcome to exact your revenge anytime now."

Nico fought for his next breath of air as Lainie settled against him to watch the action unfurling for the camera. Leaving him hot and horny and frustrated. And very ready to take that revenge, curse the woman.

Sensual scenarios rolled through his mind while Bram and Rosaria danced around the suite in a slow swirl. Nico had missed the first few lines, but he didn't miss Bram's hand squeezing the actress's ass just the way Nico wanted to squeeze Lainie. And Nico caught the dark shadows in the actor's gaze that probably looked like intensity to another observer, but which

Nico knew damn well was anger and frustration and a fervent wish to be with another woman.

Damn but that sucked.

Nico, in the meantime, had exactly the woman he wanted in his arms right now. Would he be so stupid as to turn a blind eye to what he really wanted? To let this woman slip away when he was dying for her?

His gaze locked on the couple's joined bodies, he knew he'd never survive this kind of torment with his honorable intentions intact. He wondered why he even bothered when fate was pounding on his door with both hands. All this time he'd been telling himself that he couldn't afford to become emotionally entangled with a woman he already cared about, but seeing the hot frustration etched in Bram Hawthorne's expression made Nico realize he'd be an idiot if he didn't act on what he really wanted.

Lainie.

"I call it a poor substitute for what we'd both rather be doing." Rosaria's throaty voice echoed Nico's thoughts.

"Never let it be said I cheated you out of what you really wanted." Bram halted their dance altogether, his hand moving possessively up the heroine's arms, over her shoulders.

Nico saw his own hands on Lainie. His fingers dipping beneath the fabric of her neckline to trace her breastbone down to the valley between her sweetly sloped breasts. To plunder under the cups of her bra and hold those soft mounds in his hands.

Just the way the hero was touching the heroine right now.

Nico would have grabbed Lainie and bolted if it wouldn't have disrupted the filming. He'd been off his rocker to think he could stay away from her. Hell, this heat between them, this undeniable chemistry that blasted through his veins right now, was worth every risk.

So what if he got his heart checked and slammed into the boards for all the world to see? Wouldn't be the first time. Unlike her, he didn't care so much about what other people thought.

Wondering how he'd make it through the rest of the provocative vignette, he decided it wasn't too soon to start exacting that sensual revenge Lainie had goaded him with. While Bram and Rosaria tore off one another's clothes in a brand-new kind of dance, Nico closed the distance between him and Lainie, pressing up against her from behind.

She stiffened for a moment, no doubt wary of the other guests taking in the performance. No one was that close to them, but Nico backed them up a few feet anyhow, shuffling them quietly to the back of the room so that he leaned against one wall.

Her body relaxed into him now that their closest neighbors were several feet away and obviously watching the love scene with rapt attention. Nico's gaze flicked to the set in time to see Rosaria jump up into Bram's arms, her skirt riding high as her legs locked around his waist. They weren't naked, but close. Her bra remained, the straps dangling. His shorts were still there, his pants on the floor.

But Nico had his own love scene to initiate, and one devilish diva that needed a bit of undressing. He studied the long hemline of her skirt and the close-fitting top, pondering how to make his move.

The zipper on the back of her beaded blouse called to him, urging his fingers closer as he leaned in to bury his face in the clean scent of her shampoo. Lowering the tab silently in the darkened room, he reached beneath the garment to find her skin hot to the touch. Did he do that to her?

Sliding his thumb beneath the clasp of her barely-there bra, he savored the soft feel of her before slowly unhooking the frothy piece of lingerie. Did he hear her swift intake of breath, or had it been Rosaria who was now backed up to the closet door? Bram leaned into her on the set, the couple making all the right motions for believable, against-the-wall sex.

The door loomed only a few feet away from where he and Lainie stood. Only that meager space kept him from taking her upstairs, or anywhere else private for that matter. He reached deeper into her blouse, his blood pounding in his head so hard he couldn't hear himself think.

Not that he was doing much thinking right now.

Skimming his hands around her ribs to the front, he cupped her full softness, savored the silken weight of her breasts. Lainie arched back into him ever so slightly, her sweet ass wriggling against him as if to remind him he wasn't the only one who could cause sensual torment here.

Wasn't that the truth? He took a deep breath in the hope of maintaining some oxygen somewhere in his body while he grazed the hardened tips of her nipples.

Biting back a groan, he was just reaching for her zipper again, to expose a little more Lainie to his gaze when the director shouted.

"Cut!"

Disappointment halted him for only a second and then, realizing he'd gotten exactly what he wanted, Nico hustled Lainie in front of him and got the hell out of there.

13

DAISY DECIDED SHE'D gladly start a Lainie Reynolds fan club if it meant she could get the hell out of jail. The lawyer Lainie recommended had given her some great advice, but hadn't been able to waive bail. Now, staring at the odd assortment of down-on-their-luck females sharing her temporary cell, Daisy heard the biggest wake-up call of her entire life.

Time to grow up, little girl. No more blaming anybody but herself for her problems. And that included Lainie, her mom, her dad—everybody. It was her own damn fault she was in here right now instead of wrapped in Bram's incredible arms, absorbing the warmth and sincerity in his gorgeous silvery gaze.

A gaze that lingered on her this very minute.

"Bram?" She shook herself, wondering if the stale pot smoke wafting off the woman sitting next to her had the power to make her hallucinate. Because there was no way a rising movie star would bother with her after what she'd done.

He put his fingers to his lips to hush her while a female prison guard yanked open the door of the holding cell. Freeing her.

Her heart swelled with emotions even though she didn't deserve to be walking out of jail. Into his open arms.

That didn't stop her from stealing the strength of his

hug for just a few moments, however. She buried her face in the warmth of his cotton T-shirt, savoring the male smell of him that had become familiar so fast.

He held her, stroked his fingers through her hair.

"Come on." He nudged her forward, away from the smelly cell where she'd been sitting in close confines with too many drunk and sweaty bodies for hours. "I'm bailing you out."

"No. I can't let you do this." She forced herself to step back before she changed her mind, before she could cave in to the selfish part of her that wanted nothing more than to follow him out of here and away from the garish fluorescent lighting. "I can't let you spend a single cent on me, Bram. I'm guilty."

There. She'd said it. Admitted her inner bitch was alive and well and writing mean-spirited "to do" lists.

Knowing she'd find condemnation in Bram's eyes, she was surprised to find mild amusement.

"You did what? Vented a little frustration on paper? Since when was that a crime?" He gave her another nudge away from the jail cell full of hookers, gang members and drug dealers who kept their eyes on Daisy and Bram.

Well, mostly Bram.

She stood her ground. "I mean it. You can't spend hard-earned money to spring me. I wrote those notes, Bram."

"Hard earned? Honey, I spit out the words someone else writes and take home a ridiculously fat paycheck because I inherited a few good genes from my folks. Some frigging hard work." He tugged her hand harder this time, hauling her with him away from the jail cell.

"You're out of here."

"I'll pay you back. I promise." Her voice broke at

the thought of him helping her out this way. How could he trust her when he barely knew her? Daisy followed him down a narrow hallway and through a steel-reinforced door only because the lady prison guard glared at them as if she'd personally beat them both with her nightstick if they didn't hurry up. "And please don't downplay your talent. You bring entertainment to people who need escape. What you do is important, even if you don't realize it."

He grumbled something unintelligible and hurried her through the police station.

"Besides, the fact that you could afford to spring me doesn't take away the fact that I made this mess myself because I was being immature and mean-spirited to write a bunch of stupid stuff about Lainie." She dodged a pair of cops escorting an old man wearing a trench coat that had been duct-taped shut. "I can't let you take responsibility for me when I'm the one who screwed up."

Bram stopped beside a row of abandoned industrial desks that were probably busy during the day. "Fine. Then how about this—*I* need you with me tonight. And as a spoiled, selfish product of Hollywood culture, I'm going to get what I want. If you don't want to be with me, that's your prerogative. But I'll be damned if I'm going to let you go back in that jail cell tonight because the fact of the matter is—I don't want you there."

The dark heat in his gaze caught her by surprise. As did the anger. The raw emotion.

She'd been so caught up in her own drama, maybe she'd missed out on some of his, because she had no clue where any of this was coming from. Nodding shortly, she allowed him to lead her out of the police station and into a quiet parking lot populated only by a few squad cars and Bram's Mercedes.

"Very well then. Thank you. And I appreciate the break." Skirting around a street lamp, she decided to be low-key until she could get a handle on what was up with the man who'd impressed her as such a nice, even-tempered guy the past few days.

"You're welcome." He pulled open the passenger door to the sleek SL55 and waved her inside. "I don't mean to be an obnoxious jerk about this, but it sucked doing my scene tonight without you there. Lainie told me if I followed you to the police station it would only ensure your presence on the front page of the paper tomorrow. Even though I knew she was right, I hated staying away from you when all I wanted to do was make sure nobody hurt you." His silvery eyes turned steely as he stared down at her. "Nobody hurt you, did they?"

Surprised by a level of fierceness she hadn't expected, she simply shook her head.

"Good." He hustled her into the car before anyone noticed them, then jogged around to the driver's side door to settle into the rich leather interior beside her. "You'll think I'm a nutcase, but I felt a connection between us last night that—aw, hell. I don't know. You and me together, it just worked."

She knew. Of course she knew. As Bram put the car in drive and pulled out of the parking lot, she just couldn't bring herself to believe he felt the same way. Since when did a movie star feel connected to her, the high-school dropout with a reputation for being every bit as fast as Bram's sporty car.

"I thought it worked, too, but I was afraid it was only me who felt the earth move and all that." She reached a tentative hand across the plush leather console that divided them, the sleek barrier reminding her she was a trespasser in his fast-track, glitzy world.

What could she ever offer a guy like Bram?

On the other side of the console, Bram resisted the urge to close his eyes and soak up the gentle warmth of Daisy's palm against his cheek.

"You weren't the only one." His words seemed too stark, too barren for what she deserved to hear. Why hadn't he paid better attention when the heroes he played were professing undying love for their women?

All right, so it was too soon for undying love. Maybe undying optimism. A certainty that if they worked at this, they could find something real and lasting. Something that wasn't a synthetic Hollywood gloss-over. He didn't want this to end when he had to leave South Beach. He wanted Daisy with him, keeping him balanced.

Too bad she was already retreating to her side of the car. She still wore his sweats and the UCLA T-shirt he'd given her after they'd made love last night. The clothes and the big black leather seat emphasized her petite stature, her delicate features.

"That's all the more reason why I don't want you to get caught up in the mess I've made of things." She flicked a strand of bright blond hair from her eyes. "You're too nice to be mixed up with a girl who's got a past and may soon be acquiring a rap sheet. You've got a reputation to protect and a growing box-office value to consider. For all you know, I could be a gold digger in addition to being a vindictive note writer."

Bram swerved the Mercedes out of traffic and screeched to a halt at the end of MacArthur Causeway. "*Are* you a gold digger?"

"It just so happens that I'm not, although I'd be lying if I didn't admit the stardom attracted me almost as much as the rest of you at first. But I've learned a few things about myself—and you—since then. And now I can tell you, in all good conscience, that all I'm really interested in is *you*. But how can you take my word for it?"

Taking deep breaths, he processed her words and hoped like hell she meant them.

"Easily. Because I suck at managing money and I've got less than nothing to my name." He would just come clean here and now and get it over with since she seemed so hell-bent to show him all her own flaws tonight. "Don't think for a minute you've got the lock on secrets, sweetheart, because you don't know me nearly as well as you think you do."

She raised a blond eyebrow and leaned closer like a coconspirator.

"No money?" She glanced around the interior of the luxury car. "Pretty nice toy for a man with nothing to his name."

"A gift that I need to sell before I put too many miles on it. Something I should have done the moment it was delivered, but I've been dragging my feet. The producer of *Diva's Last Dance* gave it to me as a sort of signing bonus." He clicked the car ignition into silence and whipped off his seat belt so he could face her. He prayed his admission didn't send her running, but his gut told him she wouldn't be that kind of girl.

"The only reason I'm playing the movie-star thing to the hilt is because my sister—Eileen—has some kind of undiagnosed degenerative nerve disease that's eating away at her every day. She's got no insurance, no nothing except for me, and I promised her that would be enough to make at least some sort of difference in her quality of life.''

Traffic zipped by them as they sat at the end of the causeway, the ocean shimmering in the moonlight and reflected the glow of street lamps just beyond the guardrails.

He swallowed past the dry patch in his throat. Helping his sister was the right thing to do. The only thing to do. But he would never expect anyone to share that kind of life with him—forsaking the monetary benefits of his career so that his sister might have a few more years. Months. Days.

''I'm sorry about your sister.'' She reached across the car to squeeze his hand and he found he couldn't let go. ''But I'm glad she has you to help take care of her.'' She stroked her fingers across the back of his knuckles, her gentle touch soothing old hurts inside him. ''You really don't have any money?''

''I really don't have jack shit.'' He tried to gauge what was going on behind those wide blue eyes of hers. He could practically see the wheels turning in her head before she nodded slowly.

''That could actually be good.''

''No, that actually sucks. When the rest of L.A. heads to Aspen for Christmas every winter, I'm cooking another bag of rice for dinner in a fourth-floor walk-up. But I'm happy as hell when I talk to my family and hear that Eileen is resting a little easier because she underwent a new surgery.''

''I'm sorry.'' She inched closer to him in the dark confines of the car, her expression lit by the electronic glow of the digital dashboard. ''I didn't mean to imply it was great you had no money. And it makes me all the more determined to pay back every cent of that bail money. I only meant that I can see a way to help, if you ever wanted a hand. Thanks to my champagne tastes and generic-brand beer budget, it just so happens I know how to squeeze a nickel until it screams.''

He didn't want to squelch that hopeful light in her eyes, but he couldn't help but think managing his money and his sister's bills was a far cry from balancing a personal budget. Still, she must have seen a hint of his skepticism since her shoulders straightened.

''I realize I'd have a lot to learn but I'm already registered for some on-line business courses this fall, anyway. And in the meantime, I can tell you you've got to sell this car ASAP because these things depreciate like crazy as soon as you drive them off the lot. If you want, I can help you find a buyer in town while you're finishing up your movie.''

He didn't need the reminder that he'd be leaving South Beach soon. Not when his emotions were still too close to the surface after a hell of a day. Acting had the power to leave him raw on the best of days, but combined with everything going on between him and Daisy... Damn.

''And maybe if you couldn't sell it here, you could always come to L.A. with me and sell it there,'' he said.

Her eyes widened, cartoon style.

He shrugged, hoping he didn't sound as if he had too much riding on her decision even though he did. ''Because there are a lot of potential buyers in a city like L.A. I just haven't had time to find them.''

Her gaze narrowed. ''You want me to come all the way to the West Coast with you, just so I can sell your car?''

''Or so you can take on-line courses at my house.

Did I mention I have a high-speed Internet connection? You've got to have that.'' Braving a glance at her again, he could tell by her pursed lips that he was falling damn short of a hero proclaiming undying love. Unwilling to go back home by himself now that he'd found the right woman, Bram took a deep breath and got ready to bare his soul. ''Besides, I really want you there with me.''

''You do?'' The breathless note in Daisy's voice served as a standard tool for any actress who wanted to show emotion.

But Daisy was no actress. Had he finally reached her?

''Yes. I do. I can't promise you much beyond rice from a box and high-speed Internet, but I *can* promise that you'll have a fourth-floor walk-up as long as you want it.'' *Keep going, chump!* Bram's sense of timing told him he hadn't made a strong enough argument yet. He needed more weight behind his case. No wonder they paid him to speak other people's words since he sucked at coming up with the right ones himself. ''For that matter, you can always access those on-line courses from my laptop, so you could come with me when I have to travel to shoot films. And it goes without saying, you'd have me for as long as you wanted me, too—''

Daisy launched herself over the leather console and into his arms before he could finish. And although she seemed to be giggling and crying at once, he gathered that she was saying yes by the way she kept nodding.

Yes.

In spite of his bumbling attempts to get the words right, she'd said *yes*. Bram wrapped his arms around her and hauled her into his lap, already making plans to bring her back to Mississippi so she could meet his sister. As he kissed her, he wondered if maybe he had a career as a scriptwriter ahead of him after all.

LAINIE DIDN'T KNOW WHAT had changed Nico's mind after all, but she wasn't about to question him as she let them into the Roman Retreat.

Sex loomed in her future—hot and intense—and she refused to do anything that might jeopardize the mind-blowing orgasms she deserved. Thankfully, Nico didn't seem in the mood to talk as he hooked his finger in the open V of the half-undone zipper at her back.

Reeling her closer, Nico dragged the zipper the rest of the way down, loosening her blouse until it fell to the plush carpet on the floor. Her bra still unhooked from their encounter on the movie set, Lainie smoothed the skinny straps off her shoulders, allowing the garment to slide off as she sank back against Nico's chest.

Delicious.

She'd be willing to bet more than a few female fans had drooled over his athlete's body, yet she had the privilege of molding herself to him tonight. He raked his T-shirt up and off as he pulled her deeper into the room with him, his arm belted around her waist to maintain body contact at all times.

The Italian-inspired suite glowed with the light of electric candles from the sconces on the walls. She purposely hadn't turned on the overhead lights since the warm cast of the candelabra transformed the suite into a sensual paradise.

Caught up in her own wants, she didn't realize where Nico had been steering her until she came face-to-face with herself in an antique mirror hung above the couch. The sight of her half-naked body failed to shock her, since the woman in the mirror looked damn good at the moment. Apparently the promise of sex acted as some kind of beauty potion because the hard angles of her face seemed softened, her cheeks flushed pink as her wanton alter ego tipped her head back against Nico's impressive chest.

And had she thought she needed to diet last week? Ha. With Nico's thick forearm banded about her waist she looked practically delicate.

Suddenly aware of her absurd bout of narcissism, Lainie's eyes searched out Nico's in the reflective glass. Found his dark gaze fixed on her with even more fascination than hers had been. He ran his tongue along the top of her shoulder and into the curve of her neck, his eyes never leaving her reflection.

The woman in the mirror shivered along with her, seduced by the sublimely sexy Mediterranean male behind her. Liquid heat swirled through her veins as Nico's hands skated over her belly and peeled down her long skirt. She reached behind her to finish undressing him, too, ready to see his muscular thighs shadowing her hips in the mirror.

By tugging down his black track pants, she exposed his legs on either side of her, but she couldn't see the rest of him because he stood directly behind her. She felt him, though. As he stepped out of his clothes, the velvety length of him nudged her bottom, eliciting a sigh of anticipation from her lips.

She reached for him, but he caught her hand first, his grip tight around her wrist despite the gentle way he held the rest of her.

"Just this once, I want it to be all about you." He held her gaze in the mirror as he moved her hand to cup her breast.

The soft touch of her own fingers surprised her. Spying the world of want in his eyes, she circled the rosy nipple, her movements guided by her own desires.

"If it was all about me," she whispered back, rocking her hips slowly to keep his attention. "Your hands would be doing this right now."

She rolled the nipple between her fingers, taking deep delight in his throaty male groan. Sensing the wealth of sensual possibility in this game, she worked her hands over both breasts with slow deliberation, watching him all the time to see what he liked best.

To make sure she had his complete, undivided attention.

"You know what else your hands would be doing?" She turned her head sideways to kiss his neck, to flick her tongue over the strong column of his throat.

He lifted her hair away from her ear and kissed the lobe. "Show me."

Skimming her palms down her ribs and over her hips, she inched her fingers beneath her white-lace panties and scooched them down.

Little. By. Little.

Nico's growl came as no surprise, nor did his forceful yank of the delicate lace. She was naked and trembling with want when he spread her thighs wide with his knee, bending her forward to lean on the couch.

Oh.

Her fingers bit into the upholstery, her legs quivering beneath her as Nico rolled on a condom and arched his big body over hers. Entered her slick passage in one hot stroke.

She couldn't watch the scene before her eyes or she'd fly apart. The view was too vivid, too hot, too blatantly sexual. Instead she lowered her gaze to where her hands gripped the back of the couch, her red nails digging deep into the caramel-colored fabric. And beyond that she could see Nico's hands on her hips, steadying her for every breath-stealing thrust. Something about those strong hands on her made her weak-kneed. The way he held her tight but never too hard...

For some reason that small manifestation of his thoughtfulness spoke to her more clearly than his offer to cook dinner for a resort full of guests, or his insistence on watching over her until the kitchen bomber was caught. Nico Cesare was a hundred times the man her ex-husband had been. He was the real deal. A great guy.

And he cared about her.

The thought might have sobered her if he hadn't chosen that moment to turn her around so they could see eye to eye. Her heart pounded from a combination of sex and the voice in her head that told her Nico Cesare had broken down all her barriers.

She didn't think she'd ever been so naked before any man.

"I want you, Lainie." Hard, unyielding hands cradled her face. "Only you."

The backs of her eyes burned until she blinked. Hard. She didn't want to think about how she'd been duped in the past. And she sure as hell didn't want to start thinking maybe she could trust another man—Nico—again.

"You're not fighting fair." She whispered the same words he'd said to her a few hours ago, wishing she didn't have to face the ghosts of old demons tonight. "I only wanted—"

Sex? His body? Mind-numbing release?

All of it sounded trite in the face of what his eyes were offering her right now. Wholeness. Healing. A second chance.

If only she wasn't too scared to take it...

14

How could a woman so fearless in business be so scared when it came to matters of the heart?

Nico recognized the retreat in Lainie's eyes even while her hands reached for him, her whole body on fire from his touch. Frustration kicked through him along with renewed determination to make her feel what he was feeling. To reach past all those old hurts of hers and show her what they could have together if she was only willing to try.

Pulling her close, he kissed her. Communicated with her in the one way he knew she'd listen. His hands threaded through her silky hair, cupping the back of her scalp as he angled her head beneath his. She sighed into him with her whole body, her curves molding against him as if she'd been made to fit him. Couldn't she tell how perfect they were together?

He wanted the hot sex, too, but he'd known as soon as they'd touched one another outside on her balcony that there was more going on between them than that. His arms around her, Nico walked them backward toward the couch. Lifting her up, he laid her down on the soft upholstery.

She was so perfect for him. She reached up to pull him on top of her and he marveled how a woman so conscious of how she appeared in public could be so perfectly uninhibited with him in private.

Surely that was a good sign for their future together. A future she didn't want to give him, but one he was determined to have.

He whispered words of praise in her ear, stroking his hand up the inside of her leg. He teased one finger along the juncture of her thighs, felt the coiled tension in her as he spread her wide.

So hot. So wet. And all for him.

Lining himself up against the sultry center of her, he sank deep inside, reveling in her soft cry of fulfillment as she pulsed around him with her release. He caught her moan with his kiss, savoring the vibrations of her throaty hum against his tongue.

He held himself back, concentrating on that kiss of hers so he didn't lose himself in the exquisite squeeze of her orgasm around his cock. In his logical mind, he knew that giving Lainie multiple orgasms wouldn't make her fall in love with him.

But it couldn't hurt his case, either.

After the last lush muscle contraction subsided, Nico started the slow build again. Taking his pace down a notch, he moved inside her with deep, thorough strokes. He cupped her breasts and drew on the hard peaks with his mouth until her breathing picked up again, coming harder and faster with each swirl of his tongue around the taut nipples.

Her fingers scratched lightly across his back, her ankles locking around his waist to keep him close. Blood pounded relentlessly in his head and all through his veins until he didn't stand a chance in hell of holding back any longer.

Pressing his thumb into the patch of damp curls between her thighs, he found the swollen peak he sought. He circled. Paused. Circled again.

And he didn't have a prayer of containing her cries this time. Lainie screamed with the force of her release, locking her arms around his neck as her body bowed with the force of those sensual spasms.

He came with a force that left him light-headed, his every sensation focused and concentrated on the powerful exchange between them. The heat they generated seemed to fuse them together, binding their bodies the way he wanted to bind their hearts.

And to hell with caution, he blurted out the lone thought in his head.

"I know you won't believe me, but I love you, Lainie Reynolds."

He knew as soon as he put the words out there that it had been a mistake. He should have waited. Should have exercised more caution before laying himself on the line with a woman who'd been burned before. Her initial shell-shocked expression told him all that and more, but it didn't compare to the slow skepticism that took its place.

"You couldn't possibly." She smoothed an errant strand of hair from her face, and although he'd come to recognize that unconscious gesture of hers as a common occurrence, tonight marked the first time he could remember actually seeing a hair out of place.

For once, Lainie was tousled and messy as she lay sprawled on the couch in the Roman Retreat, her perfectly groomed facade erased by the beauty beneath that attracted him even more.

"What do you mean, I can't possibly? That's like me telling you that you couldn't have possibly felt either of those rocking orgasms just now. You can't refute someone else's feelings." And just how he became the sensitivity expert in this relationship, he had no idea. The guys on his team would laugh their asses off at the thought of their maniac goalie coach preaching to his girlfriend about getting in touch with her emotions.

"I'm sorry." She skimmed her hands over his chest in a fluttery gesture that sent a shiver up his spine. "I'm just a little caught off guard."

"And scared as hell." He hadn't meant to say it, but the words jumped out of his mouth as he rolled to one side of her, balancing himself on the edge of the couch so they could face each other.

"You have to admit I have good reason to be scared." She drew circles on his chest with one red fingernail, her gaze focused on the motion. "I know you're nothing like my ex, but I can't see myself making a big leap of faith and trusting another man after what he put me through." The hand on his chest curled into a fist. "And he wasn't even a professional athlete complete with groupies. I can't imagine how many women flock to your team during hockey season, and I would hate being jealous of every female fan just because some slimeball screwed me over in the past."

"You think I haven't been screwed over in the past? Damn it, Lainie, it hurt like hell when Ashley turned out to be interested only in the fame and fortune. But more importantly, do you know how many fans I've slept with over the course of my career?" He covered her tightened fist with his palm, closing his hand over hers.

"I don't want to know that." Her eyes widened in obvious horror.

"I'll tell you how many."

She shook her head and hummed loudly as if to cover up anything he might say.

"One." He shouted to be sure she could hear him. She stopped humming. "One?"

"Yes. And that happened to be the same woman I was going out with when my career ended. The same woman who didn't give a rat's ass about me when push came to shove. Want to know how many women I've slept with my whole life?"

"Please let's not share numbers like this. Every woman's magazine ever published says it's a bad idea to share too many specifics about past bed partners."

"In your case it's necessary because of extenuating circumstances in your past. But how about if I just tell you that, even including you, I can still count every intimate relationship on one hand."

"Really?"

"I'm not some player out to score as often as possible, and if you knew anything about my family or how I was raised, you'd understand why. I have too much respect for women." His father would have pounded his butt if he'd chased a woman just to get her in bed.

"I do remember Giselle bemoaning how overly respected she was, now that you mention it." Lainie smiled, her fingers relaxing against his. "I think that's why she ran away to Club Paradise. So she could put a little sizzle in her life."

"Right. And now that she's found it, we're just waiting for the news that she's going to get married and live happily ever after with this guy. I'm giving her three more months to live with this guy overseas and then I damn well better hear some engagement news."

"That's incredibly old-fashioned. And chauvinistic."

"But it's the same standard I hold myself to. I

wouldn't mess around with anybody I didn't care about. Deeply.'' He pressed his suit with the same relentless approach that had always given him an edge out on the ice. ''But it goes even deeper than that with you. I lo—''

Lainie shushed him with a finger over his lips, her eyes pleading for him not to repeat the sentiment she wasn't ready for. ''Please wait. I just don't know how I feel about everything, and it wouldn't be fair to rush into something unless I'm certain.''

Wait? ''And it wouldn't be fair to you if I didn't let you know that I suck at being patient. The best I can do is try, but I don't know how successful I'll be when all I want to do is make love to you for the rest of the night and know that you feel it in here—'' he smoothed a hand across her chest, just above her heart ''—as much as you feel it everywhere else.''

He had the whole night in front of him, and he planned to use every minute of it reminding this woman just how good they could be together.

LAINIE HAD FORGOTTEN what it felt like to wake up next to a man.

Even before she opened her eyes she was aware of the warm thigh slung over hers, the bristly arm curved protectively around her waist, the scent of Nico's aftershave on her pillow. Then again, she'd never awoken to find her ex-husband still holding her in the morning—she and Robert had both brought serious space issues to their marriage.

Nico, on the other hand, didn't seem to have any such problems. He wore his heart on his sleeve as prominently as his team logo and didn't care who knew it.

After prying one eye open, Lainie stared across the pillow at the man who had flipped her world and her space issues on their ear. While awake, she'd never given herself permission simply to look her fill because God forbid she communicate too much attraction.

Now, at her leisure, she took in the stubborn jaw shaded with bristly dark hair. His powerful shoulders propped the bed sheet up high, creating a mountain of man and muscle, his bronze skin contrasting deliciously with the creamy white linens.

No question, waking up with a man in your bed ranked right up there next to double-fudge ice cream or the full-service manicures that included a dip in warm paraffin wax. But she'd never been a woman who indulged herself, even under the best of circumstances. And since Robert had betrayed her in every way possible, she'd retreated even further behind a wall of cool business practicality.

Even if she trusted in Nico's old-fashioned code of honor and believed he'd never cheat on her, how could she ever trust herself to make things work with this incredible man? Perhaps part of her had always feared the reason Robert cheated on her was that she allowed their marriage to fall into a pattern of cool distance and well-defined boundaries. True, her ex was a slimeball no matter how she sliced it, but what if he'd been driven to cheat because she'd made a really lame wife?

Frankly, Nico deserved better than that. And she hated the idea of him waking up beside her one day and realizing she wasn't the together, accomplished woman she appeared on the outside. She was a mass of personal insecurities that she hid very effectively beneath her professional successes. She identified with the wizard of Oz at the end of the movie—a big honking presence behind the safety of his curtain, but a serious goofball once Toto uncovered his hiding place.

"You're not going to give me a chance, are you?" Nico's scratchy morning voice startled her, his dark eyes now open and very much focused on her.

Stanching the urge to dive beneath the covers and wake him up with the same kind of sexual favors they'd traded all night long, Lainie forced herself to meet his gaze.

"I'm afraid to give *me* a chance." She wanted him to know where the real fault lay.

"Same thing, isn't it?" He propped an elbow on his pillow, his thigh sliding off hers beneath the sheets. "Either way we end up apart when it would have been a damn good idea to stick together."

She hadn't been prepared for the frustration in his voice. The anger. But then, Nico was obviously better versed in a whole range of emotions she didn't allow herself. Maybe it only made sense that a man who could fall in love so fast could also be quick to anger or quick to feel joy.

Which only reassured her she was making the right decision by walking away. Even if it hurt like hell.

"I don't want to pretend I've healed after my marriage when I haven't, and I think you deserve a woman who can love you with her whole heart. Especially after what happened with your former girlfriend." She weighed the words carefully, hoped he'd understand.

"Don't you mean that you're just too scared to try?" The edge in his voice put her on the defensive when she'd wanted to be understanding.

"If I was scared, I would have said as much." She tugged the sheet closer then wound a corner of the fabric around her finger. And felt all her own defenses kick into overdrive.

Nico slid out of bed, leaving her wrapped in the covers alone. He stepped into his pants and glared at her.

"Fine. Deny it all you want. But I want you to consider something." He yanked his shirt over his head and slipped on his shoes. "If you ever decided to put half as much energy into your personal relationships as you pour into this business of yours, you might be a whole lot happier. You know what they say about all work and no play, don't you?"

She bristled. "Are you calling me dull?"

He raked a hand through his hair. "No. But I still stand by the accusation that you're scared, and I think that's a piss-poor reason to miss out on something that could have been really good."

She waited for him to walk out so she could indulge the tears that stung the corners of her eyes. But damn his arrogant, know-it-all hide, he continued to stand there.

"Feel free to go any time now." She couldn't even work up the necessary energy for the diva death stare since right now she felt too drained and too miserable and too worried that Nico was right.

"Just because I'm mad doesn't mean I'm going to ignore my promise to look out for you. In case you've forgotten, someone may still be out to get you if Daisy Stephenson isn't your kitchen arsonist."

Lainie blinked hard to banish all threat of tears, then hauled herself out of bed, sheet wrapped around her like a messy toga. "You mean now you're stuck with me even though you think I'm a coward?"

"Don't feel bad. At least you're not a dumbass who

blurts out his every thought and feeling.'' He backed toward the bedroom door. ''I'll be out in the living room and then we can go down to the taping together.''

Heart aching far more than her sore muscles from the most enthusiastic sex of her life, Lainie sought out the shower and prayed whoever had a vendetta against her would just make their move and get it over with today. She wanted Nico to be free of his commitment to her, and she knew he'd never walk away until he was certain she would be safe.

Yet Nico and all the temptation he presented felt like more of a threat to her well-being right now than any faceless prankster. She wasn't sure how much more Nico—or heartache—she could take.

DAISY DIDN'T THINK she could take it anymore.

She'd never been a patient person and now she was stuck sweating it out in the Roman Retreat while she waited to clear the air with Lainie. And, all the while, a huge, intimidating hockey player was breathing down her neck.

''She'll be out in a minute,'' he assured her as he glared down his crooked nose at her. ''But I don't give a damn that you want to talk to her alone. I'm going to be right in the next room the whole time just in case you're the one who's causing Lainie all the grief.''

''Got it.'' She stifled the urge to be defensive, knowing damn well Lainie's self-appointed bodyguard wouldn't change his mind anytime soon. Obviously, the guy didn't know his girlfriend too well if he thought Lainie needed a watchdog.

Daisy had seen Lainie send grown men running in fear during the lean months when she'd been over-hauling the resort into a viable business. That take-no-crap strength was what had scared Daisy from her first day on the job, even while she admired the woman's grit.

Now Daisy shifted uncomfortably under Nico's scrutiny. She took deep breaths and thought about Bram until she could relax. Amazing how the thought of him could make her smile under the most trying circumstances.

"You know, Lainie is a lot tougher than she looks." She didn't know why she felt compelled to share that knowledge with the hockey goon, but the guy looked totally ready to break her legs if necessary.

"That's entirely not true." Nico Cesare, who Bram had told her was some kind of big-time hockey god, played toss and catch with a Hacky Sack while they waited for Lainie to emerge from the bedroom. "She doesn't like anyone to know it, but she's not nearly as tough as she looks."

The bedroom door jerked open and Lainie stepped into the living area, her sleek blond hair twisted into an elegant chignon that Daisy couldn't have pulled off in a million years. She bet Lainie would be able to fit in among Hollywood jet-setters with ease.

Daisy stood, grateful her wait was over. "I just came by to apologize and, if you had a minute, I wanted to explain."

"Have a seat." Lainie gestured to the couch as she stole a glance at her huge, scary boyfriend. "Do you mind if I catch up with you at the filming?"

"And leave you alone with the potential kitchen bomber?" Nico rolled his eyes, evidently not afraid of The Diva's wrath. "I don't think so. I'll be in the bedroom while you talk, but you know our code for trouble." He glowered at Daisy again.

Lainie waited for him to disappear into the next room and then waved her toward the couch again. "There's no code."

"Jesus. I heard that," Nico shouted.

"You were saying?" Lainie seated herself on a white chaise and waited expectantly.

"I just wanted you to know how sorry I am about all the trouble you are having and to let you know that, in spite of that stupid note I had in my purse, it wasn't me who planted the bomb."

"Out of curiosity, were you the one who made the chef quit?"

"Honestly, I don't think so, but I was talking smack in the kitchen a couple of weeks ago about what it had been like to work here. There's a chance what I said influenced her decision to leave."

"And even though you hated working here and want to see my business fail, you felt the need to come apologize?" Lainie folded her arms across the jacket of her formfitting blue power suit.

Defensiveness fired through her, but she tried remembering what Nico had said. Lainie wasn't as tough as she looked, right? Gulping down her shallow breaths, Daisy focused on why she came here. "I wrote that note because I like to vent on paper and somehow you'd become one of my favorite mental villains. You know how on soap operas there's always a character everyone loves to hate?"

Lainie didn't appear to have a clue about soap operas, or characters that people loved to hate, but Daisy distinctly heard Nico snort in the next room.

"I think part of the reason I fixated on you is because you're so strong and together. You're everything I wished I could be but knew I didn't stand a chance of becoming. And when you fired me—well, I was more than a little pissed." Until she'd decided to leave South Beach and distance herself from the people who didn't believe in her. Until she'd met Bram, who saw beyond who she was to who she could be.

"I know it was my fault for not doing my job. Took me a while, but I figured it out. Now, I've put myself on a self-improvement program of sorts, and I think it's important to fix some past mistakes before I forge ahead. I'm moving to L.A. with Bram next week. Starting an on-line degree program."

Holding her breath, she waited for some sort of reaction from the woman notorious for her cool demeanor. Sure, Daisy felt better about herself and her new direction in her life, but having business powerhouse Lainie's stamp of approval would be a big confidence booster.

"Sounds like congratulations are in order." Lainie's affirming nod ranked as the most support Daisy had ever garnered from a fellow female in her life. But then, The Diva's forehead furrowed. "You say this is part of a self-improvement program?"

"Yeah, like a twelve-step program for recovering screwups."

To Daisy's great surprise, Lainie laughed. Loudly.

"Let me know how it goes, will you?" Lainie peered over her shoulder at the door leading to the bedroom and lowered her voice. "I may be in the market for just such a thing one of these days. What are you studying?"

"Business." While Daisy reeled with the thought of the ultimate perfectionist ever screwing up anything, Lainie scribbled something on a sheet of hotel stationery and then tore it off and handed it over.

"Here's my e-mail address if you find yourself with business-related questions. I've expended huge amounts of energy to make myself an expert in the field, occasionally at the expense of the people in my life. Perhaps I can do a little self-improvement work on my end by lending you a hand."

Daisy blinked. Had her aloof former boss just said she wanted to help *her?* Tears stung her eyes as the import of that act washed over her. First Bram and now Lainie going out of their way to be nice to her. To believe in her.

She knew she couldn't spend her life trying to please others, but after a lifetime of being told by her mama that she would never amount to anything, this moment tasted mighty damn sweet.

"Oh my." Lainie scrambled to her feet. She reached for a box of tissues and ripped out three before handing them to Daisy. "Please don't cry. I haven't made that much progress in the self-improvement arena to know how to comfort someone in tears."

As if to prove the point, she patted Daisy's shoulder awkwardly.

Oh, what the hell. Daisy threw her arms around her and squeezed. And even though Lainie seemed too startled to hug back, she didn't scream in horror, either.

"Thank you." Letting go, Daisy wiped her nose and smiled through her tears. "I'll see you at the filming? Bram said the ending scenes are really scary as the killer finally catches up with the heroine. You don't want to miss it."

Lainie smoothed her hand over her already perfect coif as she reached for the door. "Absolutely. I've been dying to find out who's the bad guy."

15

NICO LAUNCHED OUT of the bedroom as soon as Daisy and Lainie said their goodbyes. He'd broken up his eavesdropping time by taking a quick shower, but for the most part, he'd listened in on their conversation.

For safety reasons of course.

Just because Daisy was out of jail didn't mean she was innocent. Or so Nico had thought until he'd overheard the sharefest in which Lainie had bared more of her heart to jailbird Daisy than she ever had to him.

Lainie was already in the kitchenette, pouring some kind of green goo from a blender into a glass. She looked up as he joined her again, then stuffed a straw in the nasty looking drink and took a sip.

"There's no way that's edible." He leaned closer to take a whiff and almost keeled over. "What the hell is that stuff?"

"What is it with you and Giselle? I got nothing but grief from her over my organic health drink, too." She rinsed out the blender and finished the rest of her scary concoction. "I've got to get over to the filming today if you want to go with me. They're doing the final scene, even though they still have another week of shooting. I guess they film it out of sequence and make sense of it later. Daisy said it's going to be great."

"That was damn nice of you to forgive her so easily.'' He followed her as she moved out of the kitchen, drawn to her in spite of himself.

She shrugged as she stepped into her shoes. "She seems like she could use a break. Although landing herself a Hollywood hottie ought to go a long way toward smoothing over her troubles. Did you hear she's going to L.A. with Bram?''

"He's obviously crazy about her if you had to talk him out of following her to jail.'' And Daisy apparently loved him back. How come Hawthorne got all the luck while Nico was running in circles chasing his own ass today? Still, he'd figured out a few things while listening to the women talk. "You remember what Daisy said about a self-improvement plan?''

Lainie gave him her cockeyed half smile and Nico wondered how he could walk away from her without seeing at least one more of those rare full-power grins. Selfishly, he hoped it would take a few more days for the cops to catch the kitchen bomber so he could have a little longer to talk her around, change her mind about him.

"Kind of like a twelve-step program for recovering bad girls?'' She nodded. "I remember.''

"I was thinking it sounded like a good idea for me, too. Not the recovering bad girl part, of course. Just the concept of making myself a better person.'' He turned to open the door into the corridor in an effort to keep the conversation light. Something told him if he wanted to introduce the subject of compromise, he'd better make it sound damn casual. "You ready to go check out the taping?''

Nodding, she reached for a leather binder she used for her work papers and led the way into the hall. "I promised the director I'd be on the set today in case they need anything. Do you mind if I ask what you think you need to improve?''

"Hard to believe I'd want to mess with a good thing, isn't it?" He winked as he pulled the door closed behind them. "For starters I think I need to get over myself and my NHL career. I've spent nearly a year brooding about the hamstring injury and never competing professionally again, but I'm still coaching at the highest level. And seeing the peewee kids in hockey gear the other day made me realize how much I could be doing with my rink downtown. I should be running hockey camps in the summer instead of grousing about terminated contracts."

"You might want to investigate product endorsements or franchising opportunities, too. I don't know anything about hockey, but if you were as good as you say you were, then you might be able to trade on your name with your own line of skates, or whatever else players need."

"Good idea." He'd been impressed with her smarts the first time Giselle had told him about her business partner who was turning around Club Paradise. Now that he knew her better he found even more to admire. "No wonder you're running one of the most successful businesses on South Beach. You've got a good head for that kind of thing."

After Lainie murmured a quiet "thank you," they walked in silence for a moment, taking the stairs down to the floor where the final scene of *Diva's Last Dance* would be filmed. Apparently, there would be a chase scene down the long corridor, and the action would wind up in one of the last rooms off the hallway.

"So I guess you don't need any self-improvement." He let the comment dangle for a moment, wondering if she'd bite. He'd heard her tell Daisy that she might need a plan of her own one day, and curiosity had been burning him up ever since. "You've already got everything running smoothly here."

As he opened the stairway door out onto the corridor shoot location, however, he knew she wasn't going to take the bait.

"I guess so." Cool expression in place, she seemed anxious to join the gathering crowd and production chaos already in progress on the third-floor movie set.

Damn it.

Gritting his teeth, he watched Lainie meet with one of the movie producers who also acted as her point person for contact with the film crew. Then Nico scoped out their surroundings for any potential suspicious characters.

The Persian rugs had been taken up along the hallway, leaving a more industrial base carpet to handle the mass of people. An ice chest full of sparkling water and diet drinks acted as a watering hole for gofers and set assistants.

Daisy and Bram sat on the floor at one end of the wide corridor, their heads bent together over a big map. No doubt they were charting future travels. Adventures they would share together. He hoped they knew how damn lucky they were.

Rosaria Graham listened to the director as he talked her through the layout of the scene while big booms with microphones and cameras were wheeled around the hallway. Playback televisions were visible in one of the open doors leading out into the corridor, while a fresh-faced staffer from the lobby coffee shop wheeled in a snack cart, her ponytail swinging as she maneuvered around the milling crowd.

Other than a few guests hovering at the far end of the hall, Nico didn't see anyone unfamiliar. He decided to keep his attention focused mostly on that group while the cameras were rolling. Easy to do since he and Lainie would be stationed right in there with them.

For now, he'd just try to convince himself that he was okay with Lainie's rejection this morning because there was always the possibility she'd change her mind. And he loved her enough to wait around until she finished her twelve-step program or whatever the hell she needed to do to realize they were right together.

He just hoped she'd see things his way before they both landed in the nursing home because he knew damn well that after loving Lainie Reynolds, he wouldn't be counting off any more relationships on his other hand.

ON ONE HAND, LAINIE REALLY wanted to stand by Nico during the filming.

On the other, she wasn't so sure she could trust herself to be next to him and not tell him she was crazy about him, too.

After finishing up her brief meeting with one of the producers, she searched the busy corridor for a few square feet that weren't dominated by a certain six-foot-plus hockey player. But when you were a woman in firm denial about the possibility of being in love with a man, every facet of life conspired to remind you of that particular male.

In other words, it didn't matter whether she stood near him or not during the filming since she'd be thinking about him anyway.

Sighing, she vowed to act like a grown-up as she wound her way through the corridor, which had been dimmed for dramatic effect. By the time she reached Nico's side, the director was already getting Rosaria in place for her big scene.

''I hear we're going to have the option of following the cameras down the hall as the chase scene progresses,'' she told him. ''Apparently they're not using any audio in this section since the action will be accompanied by scary music, so it doesn't matter if we make a little noise. We just can't distract the film crew.'' In an effort not to stare at Nico, Lainie peered around the corridor and spied Bram and Daisy in a far corner, heads bent together over a map, dreamy looks in their eyes.

How was it that two people could look so right together despite all the differences in their worlds? Somehow they fit. Maybe because they had all the important things in common?

She looked back to Nico, wondering if she wasn't missing the bigger picture with him.

''Stay out of the film crew's way? Got it.'' He shoved a hand in the pocket of his red gym shorts. His white polo shirt showed off the deep bronze of his skin and made her want to walk her fingers all over his broad chest.

What if they could fit together as well as Daisy and Bram?

She gripped her leather binder tighter as the lights dimmed even further and the director called for quiet on the set. Was Nico thinking about the last time they'd watched a taping together? The dim lighting and their proximity to one another had been enough to ignite so much hunger that Lainie had actually let him unzip her blouse in public. Let him run his hands all over her, any way he wanted.

Come to think of it, being with Nico had inspired her to be more sexually daring than she'd ever been before. She'd pursued him, for crying out loud. Even after he'd told her he wanted to hold off on intimacy.

She'd always been too self-conscious of her mother's promiscuousness to allow herself that kind of sensual freedom before. Yet with Nico, she'd barely thought twice.

Amazing.

Lainie felt a lightbulb start to click on in her head as the world around her went darker still and the action sequence commenced. A lone, eerie red light shone on Rosaria Graham as she ran out of one hotel-room door into the hallway area. But Lainie couldn't concentrate on the scene with her blood pounding in her ears, her brain finally making a firm connection between her heart and her mind.

And the voice in her head shouted that the reason she'd acted differently with Nico was because *he* was different. He had nothing in common with her player ex-husband who'd been all about appearances. He'd hidden his true self from her for years. Nico, on the other hand, didn't care how he looked to the world. If anything, he'd gone out of his way to be honest with her, even if his truth drove her away.

She reached for him, needing his support as a wave of stifled emotions flooded over her.

He wasn't there.

Frowning, Lainie blinked and realized that the rest of the guests on the movie set were following the cameras down the corridor as Rosaria, pale faced and wide-eyed with terror, ran from her assailant.

Lainie moved to join them—to join Nico—when a

hand grabbed her from behind. Fingers clamped over her mouth.

What?

Confused and thinking she'd somehow stumbled into the movie action scene, Lainie moved to step out of the tall man's grip, but the guy behind her only responded by wrapping his other meaty arm around her waist. Biting into her waist with grubby nails. Dragging her away from the camera.

Away from Nico.

And while the frightened heroine of Hollywood's next sexy action-adventure ran one way, Lainie was hauled roughly the other way.

No!

Fight-or-flight instincts roared to life, but she didn't have a chance to act on either with one hairy arm wrapped around her middle and a fat palm pasted across her mouth. This could be her kitchen bomber. The person Nico had been warning her about. But she'd been too intent on running her business to listen.

Arms pinned to her side and her legs struggling to find purchase on the floor, she was yanked backward into a nearby suite. Normally, Lainie rather liked the pirate-themed Booty Boudoir, but right now she wanted no part of playing helpless maiden to some creep's pillaging buccaneer.

Nico would miss her. Find her.

"Don't even think about screaming, Lainie." The vaguely familiar voice behind her snarled as he edged deeper into the room with her. "You don't want to bring all of your Hollywood guests into close contact with my gun. Besides, a smart businesswoman like you definitely doesn't want any more negative publicity for the resort."

Lainie struggled to place that familiar voice but she couldn't see the man who held her, his big arms wrapped around her like a straitjacket.

"I only want to talk to you, understand? If I let go, you have to promise not to scream or I'll need to use the gun prematurely."

Gun?

Her stomach churned with a reminder of the organic health-food shake she'd had for breakfast. The stuff was gross going down, and she definitely didn't want a taste of it coming back up.

She nodded. Ready to agree to anything if only he'd let go of her.

Easing his hand from her mouth, her abductor moved into view as he reached for his gun and turned the weapon on her.

"Paul?" No wonder she'd recognized the man's voice. The gun-toting assailant was one of her ex-husband's lackeys, a Rat Packer who'd never been convicted because the police never had enough evidence. Paul Bertoldi had managed Club Paradise's restaurant back when the resort operated as a couples' haven. He'd also dated Summer Farnsworth long ago, before she got over her penchant for tattooed tough guys.

"Nice of you to remember me, Lainie." He cocked the weapon and jerked it in the direction of a gilded chair. "Have a seat and let me tell you what I need from you."

She sat, knowing it couldn't be good. Straining for some sound from the hallway outside, some hint that Nico was already looking for her, she cursed the heavy old architecture of the hotel that made the rooms so private and quiet.

"Robert's trial is coming up and we need you to

change your story when you testify. Recant all that bullshit about him stealing money from your personal accounts.'' Paul leaned on the back of the sofa as he stared at her over the barrel of his gun. The mermaid tattoo on his right shoulder smiled at her inanely. ''And just in case you're reluctant to lie, we're prepared to give you a little incentive. You cooperate with us and no more of your pretty hotel gets blown up.''

''How generous of you.'' Her heart pounded at the realization that this was the man who had decimated her kitchen and injured two people. ''But do you have any idea how many laws you're breaking right now by threatening me? I know you want to help Robert, but you've got to realize you're throwing yourself right back under police scrutiny by setting off explosives and attacking me.''

''Gotta pay the bills somehow.'' He shrugged his big shoulders. ''I don't exactly have job offers pouring in after hanging out with Rob Flynn. So what do you say—you going to change your story, or do you want me to start setting off the bombs I've got planted around your hotel?''

Anger roared through her. Fury with him, with Robert, with herself for marrying a man who would go to such lengths to protect himself.

Could it be true? Paul had never been the brightest bulb in her ex-husband's employ, but if Robert was calling the shots behind this, she could easily guess he would have told the guy to cover his bases and plant explosives ahead of time.

Which meant this overgrown thug could blow up a room that held one of her guests. Or Nico.

Anger turned to cold fear as the full import of a potential bomb washed over her.

"Okay. Consider my story altered accordingly. You can tell Robert I'll say whatever he wants." She could always lie now and involve the police later. Assuming this guy would go away without hurting anyone today. "Just please don't harm my guests. They don't have anything to do with this."

Paul nodded as if satisfied. "As long as we don't see any police cars at your hotel again, we've got ourselves a deal." He narrowed an eye at her until he looked like a one-eyed pirate, an ugly fixture in the Booty Boudoir. "But at the first sign you've gone to the cops about this, we'll start taking out one room after another."

Lainie gulped. Nodded. And this time, she really hoped she didn't hear voices in the corridor. She'd rather take her chances getting rid of Paul on her own than risk having Nico get involved. Or worse, having Nico hurt.

"I won't be going to the police." She'd figure out how to safely point the finger at him and her ex-husband later, when she wasn't staring down the wrong end of a handgun. "May I leave now? My friends will be wondering where I've disappeared."

"And leave me here like a sitting duck? I don't think so." He rose to his feet and then dug around in a duffel bag on the couch before pulling out a length of rope. "I'm going to put some serious distance between me and the hotel first, but you know how many friends Robert has on the outside. Someone will be watching the hotel after I'm long gone. Even if you finger me, there's no way of knowing who else Robert has waiting to take my place."

He stalked closer with his length of rope and this

time, Lainie was certain she heard voices outside in the corridor. A man yelling.

For a moment she wondered if it could be Nico, but more than likely it was part of the movie scene in progress down the hall. She hoped Rosaria managed to fight her silver-screen attacker better than Lainie was fending off her real-life menace. But she couldn't risk a fight when lives were at stake. She knew without a doubt if Nico was to stumble on Paul holding a gun to her, he'd fly at the guy with nothing but his fists for weapons.

It was his crazy, all-or-nothing goalie mentality, a fearless attitude that made him put himself on the line. And it was one of the many reasons she loved him.

Loved him, damn it.

Why did she have to wait until creepy Paul Bertoldi threatened Nico and her resort to realize what mattered most? Once again, she'd known something deep in her heart but had refused to admit it. Hadn't she vowed she wasn't going to live in denial after all those months she'd suspected her ex of cheating on her and had turned a blind eye?

Confident she was doing the right thing by submitting to whatever Paul had in mind, Lainie extended her wrists in an effort to be helpful. She wouldn't let Nico play hero for her, not when the results could be deadly.

Paul tied her to the chair lightning quick, his rope biting into her skin and pinning her arms behind her at an unnatural angle. He glanced around the room as he scooped up his duffel bag and packed away his gun.

"The knots aren't that tight. You should be able to free yourself in thirty minutes if you work quick. A couple of hours if you don't. No screaming or else I'll have to use the detonator in my bag." Patting the duffel bag, he walked backward toward the door, shoving a pair of dark glasses on his nose and a navy baseball cap on his head.

"These knots are loose?" Panic sparked inside her as she envisioned herself tied up in the Booty Boudoir for days on end. Or worse, one of Paul's fat sausage fingers slipping on the detonator and her hotel blasting to bits. "To Houdini, maybe. But *I'll* never get out of this."

He was already shoving open the door, however. Leaving her there.

She longed to hurl epithets and dire threats of retribution, but she didn't have any intention of breaking the no-screaming rule. She settled for sarcasm.

"Thanks for the memories, Paul. It's been real." Before the door closed behind him, she strained to hear any hint of voices in the hallway. Mostly, she strained to hear Nico's voice.

Instead, she heard a berserker cry and the distinct sound of a punch connecting with a human target.

A human target that groaned like a stuck pig.

Lainie couldn't see the doorway, thanks to the configuration of the suite, but she could see the top of Paul's head as he fell backward on the floor with a thunk.

Then Nico was sprinting over him and landing in the middle of the Booty Boudoir with a resounding smack of his big feet.

"Take his bag," Lainie shouted, having seen enough action flicks to know the bad guy never goes down with the first punch. "He's got a gun in there."

Nico dove for the black satchel on the floor even though Paul didn't look as if he was getting up anytime soon. Members of the film crew and the movie cast filed into the room, skirting around the body on the floor.

"He said he already has bombs planted in the hotel." Lainie couldn't bear it if Nico rescued her only to have the whole resort blow up around their ears anyway. "We need to call the police and the fire department. And maybe we'd better evacuate just in case."

Daisy handed Bram her cell phone to make the calls while an assortment of sleek Hollywood types surrounded Paul and debated whether or not he'd make a convincing tough guy on the big screen. Freeing Nico to walk her way, his hands still clenched in tight fists, even as he clutched Paul's duffel bag. A wild look lingered in Nico's eyes, and Lainie decided if she played on an opposing hockey team, she would have never tried to score on him.

"How did you know I was in here?" She couldn't imagine how Nico had known to go after Paul. He hadn't been around the hotel when it had been run by Miami's Rat Pack.

"I heard you." His gaze softened as he looked at her. His touch gentle as he knelt beside her and worked free the knots around her wrist. "I was going insane out in the hallway, wondering where the hell you went when one of the doors opened and I heard your voice from inside." A hint of a smile touched his grim expression. "I have superpower hearing that can detect the diva tone at thirty paces."

She remembered her sarcastic goodbye to Paul as he'd opened up the door and marveled that Nico would have heard her.

"I was getting in my final parting shot." Her hands fell free, the blood rushing back into her fingers.

"Thank God for the diva need to have the last

word." He stroked his thumb over her chafed skin while he looked at Bram finishing up his call to 911. "We'd better get you out of here. You want me to call Summer and Brianne so they can handle an evacuation?"

She couldn't help but smile even as the adrenaline flow slowed down and left her feeling shaky. "Tell them they can have a refugee party on the beach."

Nico rolled his eyes but Bram must have overheard her because he leaned into their conversation. "You know, I'll talk to the producers, but I bet we could get some great footage with the whole place being evacuated. Everyone on the beach could have a chance to be an extra for the day."

And so, despite Nico's grumblings about her relentless need for PR, they all found themselves surf side and in front of the camera an hour later while a bomb squad went over the whole property with dogs and some kind of electronic sensors.

The ocean air seemed to wash away Lainie's residual fear from her encounter with Paul, the relentless roll of the incoming tide reassuring in its repetition. And it lightened her heart to see her guests having fun on the shore as they jockeyed for position in the quick panoramic scene the director attempted to shoot.

Nico scanned the beachful of extras from the shelter of a palm tree as he tugged Lainie closer. "You've got a knack for making lemonade with life's lemons, you know that?" Lainie pulled him farther from the crowd, having waited long enough to get him alone after her ordeal with Paul. Now that she'd seen her attacker hauled off to jail in a police car, swearing on his mother's grave that he hadn't really planted any bombs around the hotel, her heartbeat had finally returned to normal. The police had also arrested one of the girls who worked in the coffee shop after she admitted to dating Paul and writing the note Lainie had found on her desk.

"You haven't seen anything yet, Slick." She wrenched a small silver flask from the depths of her purse and extended it to him as a peace offering. "Care to share a swig with me someplace more quiet? I traded the bourbon for one of Summer's organic health-food shakes, though I can't say that it tastes great. But I've got an even bigger plan for making the best of a difficult situation and I thought you'd want to be the first to know."

Nico glanced at the flask and then back to the crowded shore. "No thanks on anything resembling health food. And I don't think we're going to find too much privacy out here. The cops will want to talk to you before they leave."

She took a swig of her new, healthy concoction, ready to share a few things with Nico. She didn't need her shot of Kentucky courage to face life today. Not with her love for Nico proving a far headier intoxicant.

"Actually, I'm not too concerned with appearances today. How about you?" She tucked away the flask.

Eyes widening, Nico drew her farther down the beach to ensure their voices wouldn't be overheard. "You know I'm never concerned about appearances. I'm all about laying it all out there, even when it gets me in trouble."

Lainie took a seat on a vacant lounger bearing the logo from the hotel next door to Club Paradise. Nico lowered himself to sit beside her, his big, beautiful body so strong and solid when she felt vulnerable.

But for the first time, she vowed to use the same

drive and determination she'd always applied to her professional life to steer her personal goals. Right now, her main personal goal was the sexy superstud sitting beside her.

"After much consideration, I've realized that I want to take a page from your book about saying what I feel." *Deep breaths. Don't think about possibly looking foolish. Or needy. Or desperate. Just say it.*

Nico remained silent, leaving the floor open for her to simply put herself out there.

Deep breaths.

"And I wondered if you would go house hunting with me." Crap. That's not what she'd meant to say. She hadn't even been thinking about house hunting, had she?

Nico looked equally taken aback, but his dark forehead furrowed. "I don't know, Lainie. Now that the police have caught Paul, you don't need to put up with my round-the-clock presence anymore."

Panic streaked through her at the thought of Nico cutting and running now because she couldn't seem to unglue her tongue.

"That came out wrong," she blurted. "My thoughts got kind of twisted because I was thinking about how to tell you I love you, and my brain was already leap-frogging ahead to how we could make it work if we tried to be together. I thought since I live at the hotel now, and I really need a home of my own, maybe you'd want to help me pick it out. Because I'm going to try very hard to make you see that I am the right woman for you after all so that one day you'll want to move in with me. Permanently."

Double crap. Had she actually said what she'd meant to say somewhere in there?

"That is, I realized today—while Paul was threatening to blow up the hotel and everyone in it—that I couldn't bear it if anything happened to you because I love you."

There. Her moment of satisfaction at having pushed the words free fizzled as fear took its place. What if he still told her that he had to leave? That he couldn't be with a woman who needed a shot of bourbon and a death threat to make her see what had been staring her in the face all along?

But then Nico's hands were on her, pulling her closer. He stroked his thumbs over her cheeks as he gazed into her eyes, his beautiful crooked nose reminding her how sometimes people's imperfections could be their most endearing qualities. She only hoped he felt the same way since she was a walking mass of imperfections.

"I love you, Lainie."

The certainty in his voice relieved all those fears and insecurities, chasing away her worries and filling her with hope.

A shadow crossed his face. "I thought I'd lose my mind when I turned around during the filming and you weren't there. I tried to stick so close to you and the one second I took my eyes off you, you were gone."

The haunted look in his eyes told her he'd been every bit as worried about her as she'd been about him.

"You told me right from the start I should have left the hotel. If I'd listened to you and let somebody else take charge, none of this would have happened." After a year of relentless work to make the resort a success, she needed to loosen the reins. "Maybe I should take a little time off this fall. Focus on my personal life for a change."

Nico's hand curled around the base of her neck, tilting her head so that she stared up at him. "You mean focus on me, right?"

"I don't know…" Smiling, she drummed her bright red nails along his shoulder. "Can you think of how we could spend a few free days?" She certainly had some ideas in mind.

"A few days? Try weeks. And yeah, I've got a few ideas." He slanted his mouth over hers and kissed her breathless.

Skin tingling with the need to be touched, the hunger to be held, Lainie drew him down on the lounger with her, their bodies entwined. "Care to give me a sneak preview of those ideas for incentive? A few weeks is a lot of time off, you know."

His hand slipped underneath her jacket to cup her lace-covered breast. "First, we're going to work our way through your top five favorite fantasy theme rooms at Club Paradise."

Desire smoldered through her, chasing away any lingering fears and insecurities. Nico *loved* her. And now that she'd stopped running from what that meant, she only needed to sit still and enjoy it.

A very heady thought.

"An excellent start to my time off," she agreed, already thinking which suites she'd want to test out with him. "But what would we do the rest of the time?"

"Well, it'll take us a little while to find a house. And then it will take us even longer to practice making those babies we both want one day, remember?"

Her heart nearly burst as he circled his hand low over her belly. She had so much to look forward to with this man.

Happy tears filled her eyes and she didn't even try to hide them. She wanted Nico to know exactly how much he touched her heart.

"Then I think I'll need a month off at least." She kissed him with all the love in her heart and all the desire in her body, until she knew they couldn't possibly continue this on a public beach. "What do you say we start practicing tonight?"

He pulled away from her, an arrogant grin on his face. "My willingness to practice hard won me a place in the NHL. It's a task I take very seriously."

Lainie's heart skipped a beat just looking at him and thinking about the future ahead of them. "One of many reasons I admire you, Slick."

He straightened her jacket as they sat up on the lounger, careful not to tip over the chair. "You know, I hear a cold day in hell is predicted in the near future."

Frowning, she tried to figure out what on earth he was talking about. "How do you figure?"

"Because sooner or later, you're going to have to marry me." He smoothed a stray hair from her eyes. "I hope you know that."

Marriage? Funny how the notion didn't ruffle her feathers anymore. In fact, the thought of Nico standing at the other end of a church aisle from her felt one hundred percent perfect.

"Definitely. Just think, we could have it at the hotel, with a big lobsterfest on the beach afterward." She tapped her chin as if in deep thought, knowing exactly how to pull his chain. "It could be a wedding and a big publicity event."

"Maybe I'll want to use it as a chance to unveil my new hockey camp. I've been taking notes about growing a successful business, you know." He pulled her to her feet and into his arms as the twilight fell around them, the filming down at the beach wrapping up for the day while the police finished their work in the hotel.

"You know what I think?"

"Hmm?" He kissed her neck while they walked back to join the Hollywood crowd cranking up the party on the beach.

"I think we're going to go down in the record books as a winning team."

Epilogue

One Month Later…

"GIRLFRIEND, YOU'RE LIVING the high life." Summer Farnsworth sat in the newly restored Club Paradise kitchen and peered down at the photos of the house Lainie and Nico had purchased earlier that day. "This place is gorgeous."

Lainie popped the bottle of champagne she and Nico bought after the closing on their house on Palm Island, just off the Miami coast. Nico had needed to make a detour to his downtown hockey rink after the closing, but he'd encouraged her to go celebrate by spending some time at the resort with her girlfriends even though she was still enjoying her month-long leave from Club Paradise.

She and Nico had their own celebration planned for later out on the balcony off the master bedroom.

"Nico likes to swim and boat and do all that water stuff, so he thought a house on one of the islands would be perfect." Lainie handed the champagne bottle to Brianne while she searched the stemware cart for long-stemmed flutes, her huge diamond solitaire engagement ring winking back at her.

Nico said he chose it because it looked like a fat block of ice. Lainie adored it because its heavy weight was a constant reminder of all the ways he made her feel loved.

Brianne filled the glasses while Lainie passed them to her. "I take it you're convinced the outlook for Club Paradise is pretty rosy if you're investing in a property like this one. It's spectacular, Lainie."

"Thank you." When the third glass had been filled, the co-owners of South Beach's soon-to-be featured-in-a-full-length-film resort raised their glasses. "To a rosy future!"

And as they drank their top-shelf champagne Lainie let herself enjoy the friendship and success achieved without worrying about what tomorrow would bring.

"I anticipate great profits from the resort now that we are up and running at full capacity since The Diva Penthouse has been revamped into a rentable suite." The look had changed, but the name remained. The updated Diva Penthouse offered specialty, made-to-order amenities, including green-only M&M's if that's what a guest requested. "But I never would have gone for this house if Nico hadn't surprised me by chunking down a big part of the down payment. He had a house on one of the other islands up for sale ever since his hockey contract fell through and he finally sold it."

Nico sprung the news on her by handing her the paperwork for a bank account with both their names on it—an account with a hefty balance already in place. She didn't need the financial boost now that Club Paradise was doing so well, but it had been a welcome gesture after the way Robert had taken her every last cent.

But then, every day she discovered new ways Nico was ten times the man her ex could have ever dreamed of being.

"Well, I've got something else we might want to toast." Summer withdrew a yellow envelope from her woven handbag, which was decorated with purple leather fringe. "I got a letter from Giselle today and she asked me to share it with both of you."

Lainie had a sneaking suspicion what the news would be since she'd talked to Nico's sister on the phone the night before. It amazed her that the woman who'd once been her sworn enemy—the woman she'd blamed for the dissolution of a crappy marriage—would one day be her sister-in-law. Even more amazing, Lainie felt really happy about that connection. Giselle squealed like a schoolgirl at the news that Nico and Lainie were buying a house together, her reaction as honest and unguarded as Nico's always were.

Lainie had learned to love that trait in Giselle as much as she adored it in her brother.

Brianne swiped the note from Summer and cast a suspicious look Lainie's way. "Am I the last to hear good news?"

Summer giggled. "You just need to get out more. The way Aidan keeps you all to himself, people might think you're one of his personal undercover missions."

Brianne raised a haughty eyebrow before poking Summer in the ribs. "And that's a bad thing?"

"That's a very good thing," Lainie reminded them, having found out the hard way how rare it was to find true, lasting love. "Considering how hellish the dating world is, I think we're all very lucky to have found the real deal."

The kind Brianne had with her unconventional FBI agent. The kind Summer enjoyed with her straitlaced politician. The kind Giselle had discovered with her idealistic journalist.

And, finally, the kind Lainie had managed to unearth for herself with a sexy jock who helped her see there was more to life than appearances.

"Spoken like a newly engaged woman." Brianne smiled, lifting her glass in Lainie's direction before she unfolded the note. Scanning Giselle's letter, she grinned even wider and then read aloud,

"So I haven't sent out the invitations yet, but I wanted you all to be the first to know that Hugh and I are coming home to South Beach for our wedding."

They all screamed. Laughed. Poured more champagne and celebrated the news of a wedding, made all the more fun because every last one of them was head over heels in love.

"What's all the commotion in here?" Nico's voice boomed through the echoing kitchen, the swinging door closing behind him as he entered. "You all make more racket than my peewee league."

Lainie smiled, her happiness automatic at the sight of the man who believed in 'til-death-do-us-part as much as her. "You finished up early at the hockey rink."

"You can afford to do that when you're the boss." He flexed that arrogant male chest that appeared to be as much bluster as muscle. "I've been trying to tell you that. You ladies work too hard when you should be having a good time."

"Speaking of good times, have you two set a date yet?" Summer asked, finding a champagne flute for Nico. "Do you have more good news to share with us?"

Nico accepted the drink as he slid an arm around Lainie's waist. Planted a kiss on her lips. "Not yet, but I'm working on it. Lainie says she needs at least six months to plan a wedding. Who needs six months? I told her I'd get some flowers, round up some friends and—" He stopped as he took in the grinning faces all around him. "Why? Who else has good news?"

Lainie pointed to the note Brianne still held. "Apparently Hugh proposed to your sister."

A whoop of joy filled the kitchen and resonated off the bare walls as he slapped the countertop so hard their glass flutes rattled. "I told him he needed to make an honest woman out of her. Damn straight they're getting married."

Summer crumpled up her cocktail napkin and threw it at him while Brianne folded her arms and shook her head in disgust. "An honest woman?"

Lainie gave him just enough of the diva death stare to make him realize he'd put his foot in his mouth. But she couldn't put much heat into her glower since Nico's habit of speaking his mind amused her far more often than it created trouble. She'd never have to wonder where she stood with a man who couldn't help but share his every thought.

And thankfully, she'd never have to worry about her ex-husband again. Even though his trial hadn't come up yet, her attorney friends all agreed he wouldn't be getting away with anything less than life imprisonment after bombing her kitchen and planting two other explosives in the resort, which the police had quickly deactivated.

Paul would be serving time, too, as well as his girlfriend who'd been working in the coffee shop. The local college girl had been Daisy's roommate one night at the hotel and she'd admitted to stealing a peek at the note Daisy had written about creating an explosive situation at the Club. She'd urged Paul to use a bomb as his scare tactic of choice and then tipped off the police about the list in an effort to finger her friend.

Some friend.

"This was the wrong crowd for that kind of comment, wasn't it?" Nico pretended to mop up sweat on his forehead. "You know what? Just for that sexist remark I'm going to personally see to it that Giselle has her whole extended family around her on her big day. I'll fly all the Italian relatives over to cheer her on when she says the vows that she doesn't need to say to make her an honest woman."

Summer shrugged. "Well, that's nice and all, but I think you should have to follow her around on her wedding day and make sure her train doesn't get stepped on."

"And you need to let her take you on a complete tour of Club Paradise to tell her how proud you are of her contribution to a successful resort," Brianne added.

Nico's shoulders slumped. "Fine. But I draw the line at going into the Fun & Games Chamber with my sister. Not going to happen in this lifetime."

Lainie kissed him, her hands missing him already. "Good enough. Let's drink to at least one wedding in our future."

Nico gazed down into her eyes, just long enough to send a shiver of anticipation through her before he lifted his glass. "To the wedding."

"And to true love," Summer added, her voice laced with amusement.

Lainie imagined her friend's giggle was at her expense since Lainie couldn't seem to tear her gaze away from Nico. The man she'd just bought a house with. And, regardless of whether or not they had a wedding planned, he was the man she'd be spending the rest of her life with.

''To true love,'' she echoed, sipping her champagne with relish.

Surrounded by her friends and the promise of Nico's love reflected in his dark eyes, Lainie was convinced the bubbly concoction had never tasted so sweet. But even though sipping champagne with Nico was fun, she couldn't help but think how cool it would be to share an occasional swig of her grandfather's home-made Kentucky bourbon with him, too. Possibly while they shared pretzels in bed.

At last she'd found a man who could love her inside and out, a man who embraced her roots as well as the woman she'd become.

As far as Lainie was concerned, that made the perfect combination.

* * * * *

*You're invited to a Cesare family
wedding...and all the sparks
that go along with it!*
SINGLE IN THE BEACH *continues!*
*Don't miss Vito Cesare's story as he
hooks up with a woman having*
HER FINAL FLING,
*Harlequin Temptation 983,
coming in July 2004.
Turn the page for a
sneak peek at Vito's tale...*

"AND JUST WHAT DID my uncle hire you to do here?"
Leaning on the kitchen counter, Vito Cesare stared at
the curvy brunette with the dirt smudge on her cheek
and made a mental note to call his uncle and ask him
what the hell he thought he was doing hiring help for
Vito without asking.

"I'm landscaping the property." Christine Chandler
turned to face him, her back against the wine cabinet
his brother had built long ago. "Your uncle said he
wanted this place to be gorgeous by the time his niece's
wedding rolls around, so I'm developing a large-scale
overhaul."

Nice of Giuseppe to inform him. How could he stay
at his house when she had the whole property torn up?
"He probably wanted to surprise me. He didn't
mention anything about me coming home while you
were working?"

"Not so much as a whisper." She rearranged a
length of ivy along a kitchen countertop, her hands
treating the delicate vine with tenderness. "Believe me,
I would have remembered that part."

No wonder she was a landscaper. She was obviously
damn good with plants. And good with her hands...

Could it be a coincidence his uncle had hired a
young woman who was superhot underneath all that
grass stain? And could it be random chance that
Giuseppe invited a woman to sleep in the house when

he knew damn well Vito would be coming home for his sister's wedding?

Not a chance in hell.

"I'm afraid I have to apologize." Setting his empty cup on the counter, Vito thought he had a better handle on this whole situation now. "My uncle is a notorious family cupid and I have the feeling that he set us up to stumble on one another like this. Since I'm way past marrying age in his book, I've apparently become his new target."

"Wait a minute." She frowned, her wide brown eyes turning a shade darker. Her shoulders straightened and her cheeks flushed pink. "Do you mean to imply your uncle only hired me as a potential hook-up for you and not because of my landscaping skills?"

"Hell no." His uncle had been raised in a culture that didn't approve of hooking up. He approved of marriage. Kids. Family. But he wasn't about to share that with this gardening goddess who looked mad enough to spit nails. Although he had to admit that the pink in her cheeks was making him think of wholly inappropriate ways to make her flush like that. "He probably just wanted me to meet some more nice women—"

"I am not a *nice* woman." The female who'd been so gentle with her ivy plant looked ready to personally take him out if he dared to suggest otherwise. "And I will sue your uncle for breach of contract if he thinks he can pawn me off on some overgrown, flashy playboy who is so far removed from nature he wouldn't know what to do with a bag of birdseed if he tripped over it."

"Now wait a minute." Vito prided himself on having more patience than his hotheaded brothers who made a habit of speaking before thinking. But where did she get off calling him an overgrown playboy? And did she have any idea what it made a guy think when a woman told him she wasn't *nice?* "I don't think we need to start launching personal attacks to solve this. I was just sharing my uncle's motivations with you."

"Well, you can tell him I don't appreciate being hired for my ass instead of my professional assets, okay? I agreed to a job, not a blind date."

And before he could think of a comeback, Christine Chandler pivoted on her heel and walked right out the kitchen door.

If that didn't beat all.

Of course, Vito couldn't help moving to the kitchen window to watch the ass in question saunter away, hips twitching with her snappy walk down the driveway. He felt a little bad for enjoying the view and the residual sparks in the air when she was clearly mad, but hell, wasn't the urge to ogle tattooed across the Y chromosome?

Reaching for the door to follow her outside, hormones kicking to life, it occurred to him he didn't feel tired anymore.

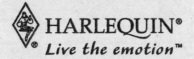

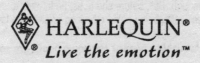

If you enjoyed what you just read,
then we've got an offer you can't resist!

Take 2 bestselling love stories FREE!

Plus get a FREE surprise gift!

Clip this page and mail it to Harlequin Reader Service®

IN U.S.A.	IN CANADA
3010 Walden Ave.	P.O. Box 609
P.O. Box 1867	Fort Erie, Ontario
Buffalo, N.Y. 14240-1867	L2A 5X3

YES! Please send me 2 free Blaze™ novels and my free surprise gift. After receiving them, if I don't wish to receive anymore, I can return the shipping statement marked cancel. If I don't cancel, I will receive 4 brand-new novels each month, before they're available in stores! In the U.S.A., bill me at the bargain price of $3.80 plus 25¢ shipping and handling per book and applicable sales tax, if any*. In Canada, bill me at the bargain price of $4.21 plus 25¢ shipping and handling per book and applicable taxes**. That's the complete price and a savings of at least 10% off the cover prices—what a great deal! I understand that accepting the 2 free books and gift places me under no obligation ever to buy any books. I can always return a shipment and cancel at any time. Even if I never buy another book from Harlequin, the 2 free books and gift are mine to keep forever.

150 HDN DNWD
350 HDN DNWE

Name	(PLEASE PRINT)	
Address	Apt.#	
City	State/Prov.	Zip/Postal Code

* Terms and prices subject to change without notice. Sales tax applicable in N.Y.
** Canadian residents will be charged applicable provincial taxes and GST.
All orders subject to approval. Offer limited to one per household and not valid to current Blaze™ subscribers.
® are registered trademarks of Harlequin Enterprises Limited.

BLZ02-R

HARLEQUIN®

Temptation

New York Times bestselling author

VICKI LEWIS THOMPSON

celebrates Temptation's 20th anniversary—
and her own—in:

#980

OLD ENOUGH TO KNOW BETTER

When twenty-year-old PR exec Kasey Braddock accepts
her co-workers' dare to hit on the gorgeous new landscaper,
she's excited. Finally, here's her chance to prove to her
friends—and herself—that she's woman enough to entice
a man and leave him drooling. After all, she's old enough
to know what she wants—and she wants Sam Ashton.
Luckily, he's not complaining....

Available in June wherever Harlequin books are sold.